The Friend Group

Ty Hutchinson

TYHUTCHINSON.COM
AUTHOR

Prologue

NOAH WAS BORN at six pounds, seven ounces. He had the cutest blue eyes I'd ever seen and a smile that never seemed to disappear. I was absolutely, one hundred percent in love with my son and excited about my journey into motherhood.

Ever since I was a little girl, all I'd ever wanted was to be a mother. Sure some people thought it was weird. And could I get a little obsessive? No doubt. But I couldn't help it. It was this unexplainable yearning inside of me that pulled me toward being a mom. I was convinced that being an only child had something to do with it.

As soon as I was old enough, I talked my parents into letting me babysit for the families in the neighborhood. I'd become so popular that school took a back seat, prompting my parents to cap me at fifteen hours a week until I graduated high school.

I never stopped dreaming about having a baby. Yes, I wanted to get married first, but I just assumed all that would work itself out. And while I dated, had long-term relationships, and experienced break-ups and heartache, I never lost sight of my goal: becoming a mother. And then I met Jake, and all the puzzle pieces fell into place. We were madly in love, and we both wanted children.

But life has a way of throwing curveballs.

When it came to pregnancies, I had drawn the short straw in life and ended up as one of those women prone to preterm labor. My pregnancy with Noah was challenging, to say the least. I had developed preeclampsia, which only magnified the stress on my body. Under the doctor's orders, I was confined to bed rest for the final three months.

Jake was my savior. He made sure I was comfortable and relaxed at all times. He could work from home during this time, even though it was difficult, and did his best to prevent me from wanting for anything. He never complained when I sent him to the convenience store late at night to buy me a bag of pork rinds and a pint of vanilla bean ice cream. I would use the rinds as spoons and thought it was the best thing ever. Jake couldn't stomach the pairing, but he still went out and got it for me. In fact, he smartened up and stocked our pantry with bags of rinds and filled our freezer with ice cream. "We're a team, Emily," he'd always tell me. He believed it was our responsibility, together, to ensure the pregnancy went the full term.

Lying in bed for three months was worth it. I was willing to do whatever it took to ensure Noah arrived healthy and safely into the world.

And he did.

When Noah was nearing the six month mark, Jake suggested a small get-together with close friends and family to officially introduce Noah to them. At first, I was against it, but not because I didn't want them to meet Noah. I had waited this long already because I was a first-time mother, and I had filled my head with so many dos and don'ts that I drove myself crazy. I thought Noah was too young and hadn't yet built up proper immunity, and the thought of having so many people holding him and giving him quick pecks on the head had me freaked out. Because that's precisely what I would have done with a newborn: I'd shower it with kisses. Who wouldn't? They're the cutest ever.

"We can explain that he's not strong enough to be held," Jake said. "He can just make a short appearance and then go down for his nap."

"I think I would feel a little guilty leaving Noah in his room while we're hosting the party."

"It's just for a couple of hours. We'll have the video monitor on Noah and can watch him the entire time."

I swished my mouth from side to side as I thought about what Jake proposed.

"We both need a break, and rest." He bent his knees a bit so his eyes could catch mine. He had that goofy smile on his face that always made me laugh. "This will be good for us. We'll have some fancy dip with chips, a few bottles of wine, and for those of us who are breastfeeding, sparkling cider. We still have half a dozen bags of rinds. Can't let those go to waste, right?"

I couldn't argue with Jake's idea for a get-together. I felt like I hadn't had a break in ages. I felt exhausted when I went to bed and the same when I woke. And I did miss seeing my parents and my friends in person. Most of my contact with them was via a video call.

"Okay, for a few hours," I said with a smile. "It'll be fun to finally see everyone."

"Of course, it will. Everything will be fine."

The following week, I left the baby with Jake while I raced around town picking up last-minute items for our "Meet Noah" get-together that upcoming weekend. I had just walked out of a party store with some cute party favors and was waiting to cross the street.

On the other side of the street, I spotted a mother with a

small child. He was full of energy as he skipped around her like she was a maypole. She focused on her phone while shaking a hand at him, urging him to grab it. I kept thinking that one day, Noah would be full of energy and would think running around me would be the best thing ever.

I pulled my phone out of my purse, wanting to capture the cuteness with a video, when the boy suddenly tripped and tumbled. Just then, a large garbage truck passed.

I'll never forget the agonizing scream that erupted on the other side of the truck. The vehicle came to a stop a few yards past the woman, but I didn't see her little boy. Where was he? Had he run back behind her? Had a passerby pulled the boy from danger in the nick of time?

The mother stood frozen in place, staring at the truck's wheels.

A scream from a passing woman echoed.

"Oh, God!" a man shouted.

"Call 911!" another person said.

I didn't need to see the boy to know his condition. A man kneeling and peering under the truck told me everything. The mother dropped to her knees, wailing. "My son!" she cried. "My son!" Another woman tried to comfort her.

I couldn't imagine what was going through her mind, but I felt her pain as my eyes welled up. I didn't blame her. We all look at our phones. We all get easily distracted. But this was a reminder to make sure my child's safety was always my top priority. It took only a few seconds for this mother's life to change drastically.

At that moment, I couldn't help but put myself in that mother's shoes. What would be going through my mind? Blame? More like guilt. Certainly, all I had gone through to bring Noah into this world, only to lose him to something so tragic. A shiver rattled my spine, and I shook the thought out of my head.

I promised myself right then I would be the perfect mother to Noah.

I would protect him. Watch over him. Keep him safe.

I hurried home, bursting through the front doors and straight to Noah's room. I picked him up out of his crib. I held him against my chest, kissing the top of his head gently as I cried, knowing I could not recover if something like that had happened to Noah because I was distracted by my phone.

"What's wrong?" Jake asked as he walked into the nursery. "Everything okay?"

"It is now. Promise me, we'll both do everything possible to make sure Noah is safe and protected every single day."

"Of course. We'll always look out for him until we take our final breaths."

I told Jake about what I had witnessed earlier.

A dumbfounded look materialized on his face as he ran a hand through his hair. "Sheesh, that's horrible. What a terrible accident...that mother...I can't imagine...."

"I don't want to be her. I don't want to be the cause of my child's death."

"You're not. You won't be. That was a freak accident."

"I know, but that's my point. How do I prevent a freak accident from harming Noah? She wasn't a bad mother. She wasn't doing anything but being a normal mother. She tried grabbing hold of his hand like any mother would, sensing that it was too dangerous to be running like that near the curb. She was calling out to him to grab her hand. She was doing her job and only seconds from grabbing his hand, when...."

My mood had plummeted, and I wanted to cancel the get-together. Jake did his best to calm me, so by the time Saturday rolled around, I felt a little better. We didn't mention to anyone what I had witnessed. Instead, we focused on our little bundle of joy.

As expected, everyone was excited to meet Noah. We explained that they couldn't yet hold him. No one questioned it, because everyone knew I had had a difficult pregnancy.

"I promise, once he's a bit stronger, you can lavish your love on him," I said.

For the time being, they settled for peeks into his crib.

Just as Jake had predicted, the party was a happy welcome. I hadn't realized how much I'd missed being around my parents and besties. We had so much to talk about and share. I don't know what it is about being with someone in person, but video calls simply can't hold a candle to it.

"Noah's so adorable," Janice said. She was my best friend and had recently gotten married. She was also excited about starting a family.

"You always hear the stories about babies developing colic, but Noah is sleeping like a champ," she said.

"You caught him on a good day," I said. "He's just getting to the point where he sleeps through the night, except when he's hungry. There was a time when I thought I would never get any sleep."

"I heard the minute you become a mom, you sacrifice a decent night's sleep," Janice said. "But Noah is the perfect baby," Janice eyed the baby monitor. "He's been sleeping soundly ever since we arrived. Even with everyone talking, he hasn't stirred."

It wasn't until Janice made mention of that it dawned on me that Noah hadn't woken since everyone arrived two hours ago. I kept expecting that he would wake from the noise and I'd have to excuse myself to comfort him. I leaned in closer to the monitor and watched Noah.

"Excuse me, Janice. I'm just going to check on Noah really quick. I'll be right back."

The Friend Group

As I walked down the hall, I couldn't shake the image of that mother on her knees, crying as she reached out for her child.

Noah is sleeping soundly. Relax, Emily.

But with each step, I picked up the pace. He was sleeping on his stomach. Usually, Noah slept on his back, and I could have sworn when I put him down in his crib I laid him on his back.

When did he flip over? And why didn't I notice until now?

In fact, I couldn't remember Noah ever sleeping on his stomach. I entered the nursery and hurried over to his crib. My senses tingled, sounding the alarm. The noticeable rise of his body from his breaths was absent.

"Noah?"

I reached into the crib, and I knew the instant that I touched him, before I even flipped him over. Just like that mother knew the moment the truck passed.

"Noooo!"

Chapter One

Five years later

Our friends and family filled the tiki-themed restaurant to the brim. They'd all come to celebrate our big move and say goodbye. In exactly one week, Jake and I would be getting on a plane and flying halfway around the world to Thailand. Jake had been doing exceptionally well at Asia Pacific Holdings, and they rewarded him with a huge promotion. Of course, the position was in Bangkok. Neither of us had been to Southeast Asia, let alone lived there. And now we were suddenly put in a situation where we were expected to pick up and leave our comfortable life in San Francisco.

Everything had happened so fast. Jake was given a week to make a decision on whether or not to take the promotion. We talked every night into the wee hours about the prospect of moving. It wasn't like he was taking a job in another state. We were moving to an entirely different country that neither of us knew anything about, nor did we even speak the language. We'd be utterly lost.

"We'll have support from my company," he said. "They'll set us up in housing and help us get acclimated." Jake grabbed my hands and held them. "We won't be tossed to the wolves when we touch down. I promise."

From the moment Jake received the news, he'd been telling me how big an opportunity it was for the both of us. Living in another country wasn't something most people had a chance to do.

"It's not a lifetime commitment," he'd said. "If for whatever reason it doesn't work and we're unhappy, we can leave."

"Are you sure? What about your job?"

"Don't worry about that. I'm married to you, not the company I work for. We'll always do what's right for us."

During the day, when Jake was at work, I Googled as much as possible about life as an expat in Thailand. I wanted to make sure we were both making an informed decision and not walking into a nightmare.

By week's end, we'd decided to go for it. The company gave us a month and a half to settle our affairs in San Francisco and move to Thailand. They were eager to have Jake out there as soon as possible. It was a race, winding down our lives and packing them into moving boxes. But we did it. And now we were holed up in temporary housing and saying our final goodbyes to the people who completed our lives in a city that Jake and I had loved for so long.

"Are you nervous?" Janice asked as she took a sip of her Mai Tai from a tiki cup. I was nursing a Singapore Sling. "You look nervous."

"I'm not nervous. I'm terrified. But I'm excited at the same time. I'm about to embark on the biggest adventure in my life."

"You got nothing to worry about. You're doing it with Jake. He's solid."

"I don't think I could have done it alone. But Jake will have an immediate ecosystem of work and colleagues' support. Me? I'll be at home by myself, having to start over."

"That's part of the fun. Think of the experiences you'll collect. Plus, that's what embassies are for. You should be able to tap into them for help, right?"

"Yeah, I suppose."

"I know I've already told you this a million times, but it's worth repeating. I'm so jealous. This is a once-in-a-lifetime opportunity. You need to dive in headfirst and milk it for all it's worth. You'll thank me later."

"Will you visit? Promise you will."

"Are you kidding? I can't wait. Just make sure you know the lay of the land before I arrive," Janice said with a smile. "Oh, and don't even think of replacing me. You can have friends while you're there, but they can't be your best friend, ever. I've already filled that position."

"I won't." I made a cross-your-heart motion over my chest.

"Do you think you'll eventually be able to work there?" Janice asked as she fiddled with the umbrella in her drink.

"I think I'll need a work permit to work legally. I'll know more once we get there."

"Well, it's not like you need to work. Jake will be making plenty of dough. You'll end up being one of those wives who spends her days either in the salon or shopping."

"Oh God, I hope not. I can't even imagine that."

"Don't knock it until you've tried it. I know you don't miss that admin job you had."

"You're right about that."

"What is it? You have that 'but' look on your face."

"Right before Jake got the news, we were talking about trying again. It's been five years since Noah's passing, and...."

"Oh, honey...we all miss Noah, but I think it's wonderful that you want to try again. And anyway, this move shouldn't determine whether or not you have kids. If you're ready, then you're ready. Just go for it."

Janice had always been my biggest cheerleader. She'd always sided with me on decisions. (Except for that one time I went through a phase when I wore berets everywhere. She'd threatened to stop being my friend.)

"You're right. I don't know why I'm letting this move be such a big factor. It shouldn't be."

Of course, the real reason I was having second thoughts had nothing to do with the move. It had to do with what happened to Noah. His death nearly destroyed me. I blamed myself and was convinced I was a terrible mother who had failed my child.

But it didn't stop there. I started blaming Jake and everyone who was at the house that day. I knew his death wasn't any of their doing, but I lashed out anyway. I was angry and hurt; all I wanted was to make someone else feel that way. Noah had died from SIDS—sudden infant death syndrome—not negligence on our part, but still, I shouldered the blame, thinking I could have prevented it. It was a tragic situation, just like the accident with that mother and her child five years ago. That promise I made to ensure Noah's safety didn't even last more than a few days. And that was something I would always live with.

The thought of bringing another child into the world and having it happen again sometimes made me nauseous. Even though I knew I wasn't to blame. Nor were my husband, family, or friends. I couldn't shake that thought.

Initially, dealing with Noah's death had been tough for us, more so for me. Mentally, I had a hard time accepting that Noah was no longer with us. My body ached constantly, my temperament was unstable, and my energy levels were nonexistent. To make matters worse, Jake and I fought almost daily. Our marriage had gotten so rocky I thought divorce was inevitable. Deep down inside, on some level, I knew I was the problem, the one who couldn't move on. For the longest time, my argument had always been, "Why do I need to move on?" In my mind, moving on meant forgetting. I didn't want to forget Noah.

But eventually, with the help of a therapist, we got through it. It wasn't easy, and it was a long and bumpy road back to the solid marriage we'd always had, but we did it. And more importantly, we'd begun discussing starting a family again. Jake worried about my mental health and would always tell me there was no rush. He believed it was important that we both be in the right mindset when we tried again. I knew he was really talking about me, but it was reassuring to hear him say "we."

The truth was, I wasn't ready, and I wasn't sure if I would ever be in the right mindset. But there was no need to ruin everything by admitting that. My heart was ready, even if my mind wasn't.

Chapter Two

Shortly after Noah's death

Client: Emily Platt
Therapist: Dr. Tammy Young
Therapy Session #: 1

Data:
Emily has indicated she doesn't think she needs therapy but is only complying with her husband's wishes to make him feel better. She says Jake thought she needed therapy because of Noah. When I ask Emily who Noah is, she tells me Noah is her son and that he's had difficulty sleeping lately, especially at night. Jake complains, but she doesn't ask him to help when Noah cries. Emily says she's always the one to get out of bed and go to him. Emily thinks Jake might be a better candidate for therapy. She states he feels abandoned and jealous that he no longer receives the same amount of attention from her. Emily tells me that she read about this condition online and that it's common with husbands. Emily spent most of the session talking about this.

Assessment:
Emily believes her son Noah is still alive and healthy, though it's been a little over six months since his passing. She doesn't speak about Noah in the past tense but rather in the present. When asked about Noah's condition, she states that he received a clean bill of health at his last checkup. Emily is experiencing a persistent, complex bereavement disorder. She's made this initial session all about her husband, and it is obvious she is only here to satisfy his nagging. Emily made no other mention of Noah during the session, nor has she admitted to experiencing grief hallucinations, as indicated by her husband. Jake has stated that Emily often mentions seeing Noah and has even told Jake that she's done things for Noah. For instance, given him a bath. Emily is convinced that any problem they are having lies with Jake.

Plan:
Continue exploring the reasoning behind Emily's feelings and why she believes Jake's jealousy is why she's in therapy and not because of the loss of her child.

Chapter Three

It was seven in the morning, and we were touching down in Thailand at Suvarnabhumi International Airport. Any apprehensions I'd been experiencing beforehand had been forgotten. I was excited to be in Bangkok, the city I'd read so much about over the past month. Even Jake couldn't contain his excitement; he bounced his legs for the last thirty minutes of the flight.

But as soon as the plane wheels hit the tarmac, Jake was on the phone with his boss. I was content to stare out the window and take in the sights, which at that point consisted of nothing but another runway and a grassy field running alongside it. But the sun was shining, and the skies were blue. The flight attendant announced over the intercom that the temperature outside was thirty degrees Celsius. I did a quick conversion on my phone: eighty-six degrees Fahrenheit. Toasty compared to foggy San Francisco.

We passed through immigration without a hitch, collected our bags, and were met inside the arrival hall by a driver holding a sign: Jake and Emily Platt. According to the welcome packet Jake's company had sent to us, we were going to be housed in a gated community in On Nut, a neighborhood populated by both

The Friend Group

expat and Thai families. I initially felt let down when I discovered that our housing had already been decided. But the more I thought about it, the more I realized it was the easier route. I knew very little about the different neighborhoods and how they compared. There was only so much information online.

The drive from the airport took nearly an hour because of traffic. Jake was on his phone the entire time. *What kind of boss needs to talk to his employee the minute he lands?* I relegated myself to staring out the window at the passing scenery. In the distance was the Bangkok skyline. There were a vast number of high-rises with decorative spirals on top. One of the buildings looked crooked, as if it were made from Lego blocks. I certainly wasn't expecting that sort of bold and unconventional architecture in Bangkok. When Jake first mentioned Bangkok, I had naively assumed there would be tiny villages and huts on the beach.

When we arrived at our complex, we passed through a gate manned by a security guard. He promptly saluted our car as we drove by, which I got a kick out of. I turned to mention it to Jake, but he wasn't even paying attention. He was still locked in the same conversation with his boss.

We approached a row of single-family townhouses, and I assumed we were being housed in one of them. They looked beautiful and roomy from the outside. I knew very little about the housing setup for us. About half of my questions to the relocation coordinator at Jake's company had gone unanswered. But we drove past the townhouses, and in the distance, I saw a low-rise apartment complex—seven floors—and my heart sank.

Please tell me they didn't stick us in a one-bedroom apartment.

A minute later, the driver brought the car to a stop at the front of the building, where a smiling woman waved at us.

"Welcome to Thailand," she said as we climbed out of the

car. "My name is Ploy, and I'm the juristic manager on-site. I believe in your country, we're called apartment managers. It's so nice to meet you two."

I shook her extended hand. "Thank you. It's nice to meet you, too. I'm Emily, and this man on the phone is my husband, Jake. Work call." I shrugged.

"I'm sure you're eager to see your place. We have you on the seventh floor with a lovely canal view." She spoke to our driver in Thai. "He'll bring your luggage."

After a quick stop in the office to sign the paperwork, Ploy took us to our place. She kept talking about how spacious the apartment was, and I took that as her simply trying to make it seem better than it was. I was wrong.

"I think you'll like it," she said, opening the front door and leading the way in.

I was instantly floored by the size of the living room; an entire one-bedroom apartment could fit inside it. It had white tile floors, it was elegantly furnished, and there was even artwork on the walls already. Ploy led us out to the balcony to show off the view. It looked down on a canal lined with trees.

The kitchen was equally magnificent, with granite countertops, a sizable island, and all stainless steel appliances. The cabinets were stocked with dishware. When the relocation manager told us our place would be furnished and there was no need to bring everything we owned—clothing and personal items would suffice—I was a little skeptical. I kept thinking what she meant by "furnished" was essential appliances like a stove and refrigerator. But, again, the apartment exceeded my expectations. Various domestic appliances, including an electric can opener and coffee/espresso machine lined the countertops. And to think the relocation package still had additional funds to cover miscellaneous housing expenses. It seemed like everything we needed was already covered.

The Friend Group

"You also have a personal wine storage," Ploy said as she opened a cabinet revealing the temperature-controlled appliance.

The apartment had four bedrooms and three bathrooms, more than enough room for Jake and me. The master bedroom was spacious and bright thanks to the floor-to-ceiling windows that let in plenty of natural light. There was a king-size bed with a tufted headboard. I ran a hand across the neutral-colored linen, impressed. A bench stood at the foot of the bed, and two armchairs were arranged in the corner. Don't even get me going with the walk-in closet lined with cherry cabinetry. The ensuite bathroom? Simply to die for, with its marble floors and high-end fixtures. The walk-in shower had four showerheads, and I was determined to use them all. But the star, and centerpiece, was a clawfoot soaking tub.

"I hope this is satisfactory," Ploy said with pleading eyes.

"Satisfactory? This is amazing," I said. "I wasn't expecting this at all."

"Oh, I'm so happy to hear that. There are only two units per floor, so you'll also have a lot of privacy, as the other unit is currently vacant." She glanced over at Jake, who was still on his call, before turning her attention back to me. "Would you like to take a tour of the grounds? If not, we can always schedule it for later."

"I think we should reschedule for another time."

"Of course." Ploy handed me a business card. "Just call when you're free. You can also call that number for any problems with the unit or questions you might have later."

After Ploy left, I took the time to look over the apartment in much more detail. Jake commandeered the dining table and started spreading out paperwork as he continued his conversation, so I let him be. The other bedrooms were smaller but still roomy. I was sure Jake would turn one into an office, which left two guest rooms. One had a double bed, and the other a single. I stood in the doorway of the bedroom with a single bed. Clearly, it was meant for a child. Thoughts of my own child staying in that room popped into my head. But what was I thinking? Even if I were to get pregnant right away, it would be years before I would be comfortable with my child sleeping alone and not in my room. Had I yet to learn my lesson from Noah?

"I know what you're thinking," Jake said as he came up behind me and wrapped his arms around my waist. "There's no rush. We just got here this morning."

I spun around to face him. "I know; I was just imagining what it would be like."

"Do you like the place?" he asked.

"Like it? I love it! It's incredible."

"Good," he said with a smile before kissing me on my forehead. "If you're happy, I'm happy."

"I am. I think we'll be just fine here."

Chapter Four

THE VERY NEXT DAY, Jake was out the door before I woke. I felt a little guilty about sleeping until ten while he was at work, but the way I saw it, he really wanted the job. And clearly, hitting the ground running the minute we landed made him happy.

Go get that money, sweetie.

I eventually climbed out of bed and walked into the kitchen to fix myself a cup of coffee. It dawned on me right then that there was nothing edible in the apartment besides a complimentary case of bottled water.

I know what I'm doing today.

Surely grocery shopping was something I could manage without Jake's help or the guidance of Ploy, from the juristic office. I'd gone grocery shopping a million times before; how hard could it be here?

All I need is to find a coffee shop, caffeine up, and I'll be good to go.

There was a welcome packet from the complex that had a property layout. To my surprise, we had our own Starbucks. It was attached to a small building that also housed a 7-Eleven, a hair salon, a nail shop, a small Thai restaurant, and a bunch of spa-related businesses. How convenient.

After a quick shower, I was out the door and walking toward the Starbucks. It took me roughly five minutes to get there. Sitting outside the café were groups of women.

Is this where the housewives gather?

One table had eight women huddled around it. My guess was that they were speaking Korean. Next to them were a group of Japanese women. I was familiar with how that language sounded. Farther away from the entrance was a smaller group of women engaged in lively conversation. They were too far away for me to make out their language, though they looked American. I kept my eyes trained on them, hoping one would glance my way and I could smile, but none of them did.

I went inside, placed my order at the counter, and waited. Every few seconds, I would look over at the table, hoping to catch someone's eye, but they were all too involved to notice anyone around them. I wanted to meet some of the other expat wives. Jake had mentioned that a couple of the men he'd be working with were married and also lived in our complex.

Relax, Emily, it's only day two. You'll make friends. Of course, you could just walk up to them and introduce yourself.

I could, but I'm terribly shy when it comes to doing things like that. I started coming up with scenarios of how horribly it would play out. It's stupid, I know. I grabbed my drink and made my way out of the shop, looking one last time at the group. No luck.

A taxi dropped a woman off, and I quickly jumped inside when she cleared the door. I told the driver the name of the grocery store, Big C. He nodded, and off we went.

So far, so good. You got coffee and managed to catch a taxi to the grocery store. This won't be so hard.

Twenty minutes later, the cab stopped in front of a row of

old, two-story buildings with black stains. The ground floor was lined with mom-and-pop shops, and the second floor looked residential. The photo of the Big C I'd seen in the information packet showed a modern yellow-and-white building. I figured I just needed to walk a bit.

I glanced at the meter, and only then did I realize I only had dollars on me. No Thai baht. The fare was seventy baht. I had automatically used my credit card at Starbucks like I usually did, so it never struck me that I needed to get cash from an ATM.

I took five dollars from my wallet and showed it to the driver. He smiled and snatched it out of my hand. I wasn't sure how much seventy baht was in dollars, but after waiting awkwardly for change that wasn't coming, I climbed out of the car.

I stood on the sidewalk looking for Big C signage. There was none. I didn't even see a large building that would house a grocery store.

This could be a smaller one, like an express version.

I spun around, looking in all directions for the store, but all I saw were shops selling motorbike parts, hardware supplies, and paint. There were a couple of small restaurants. I had to walk a bit, but which way? I had just assumed the driver knew what I was talking about when I said "Big C." I headed one way and walked for a good ten minutes, and the area turned more residential. Clearly, the wrong direction.

Just as I turned to retrace my steps, I heard barking. From the corner of my eye, I spotted two dogs barreling toward me with their fangs showing. There was no way I could outrun them, so I slipped my purse off my shoulder and started swinging it at the dogs to keep them at bay. It worked until they split off and attacked from opposite directions. My purse and I were losing the battle.

Just then, a man on a motorbike drove by and shouted at the dogs. Like clockwork, they stopped barking and ran back to wherever they had come from. If only I had known—I just needed to yell at them.

Okay, Emily, you're fine. No need to schedule a rabies shot just yet.

With my heart beating like a drum and perspiration slick on my neck, I headed back the other way. However, after twenty minutes, I still hadn't found anything resembling a grocery store.

Calm down, Emily. Just use the map on your phone and make your way to Big C.

But as luck would have it. I just remembered that I still had my old SIM card in my phone. I didn't think to get a Thai SIM card at the airport because Jake had a company phone, so it worked everywhere, and I blindly followed him out of the airport. With no internet, I walked into a nearby bubble tea shop. A young teen girl sat on a stool behind the counter, staring at her phone.

"Do you speak English?" I asked with a shy smile.

The equally shy girl smiled back and shrugged.

"Big C?"

"Big C," she nodded enthusiastically. She led me back outside and pointed farther down the road. "Big C."

I thanked the girl and kept walking. It was blazing under the sun, so my shirt was damp, and the constant patting of my forehead had used up all the tissue in my purse. About ten minutes later, I saw a large yellow-and-white building with a sign that read Big C.

Why didn't the taxi drop me off here?

Big C was huge, crowded, and muggy. If there was air conditioning, it was on low. There were no free carts, only baskets inside, so I grabbed one and started shopping.

The Friend Group

Nearly all the brands were Thai, except for one aisle where a small section of the shelving was dedicated to imports, primarily cookies, candies, and chips. I stuck to the basics: milk, juice, pasta, coffee, canned goods, bread, deli meats, condiments, and a bunch of frozen pizzas and meals. We just needed items to tide us over. Over the weekend, Jake and I could go together and do a much larger haul. I found the freezer section and stood between the door and the shelving of frozen vegetables much longer than needed, just to cool off.

Clearly, my body had yet to acclimate to the humid weather, because no one around me appeared to be sweating. While I shopped, I kept an eye out for an ATM but didn't see one inside the store.

When I got all I could carry, I stood in what I thought was the checkout line, only to discover it was a line to sign up for a local bank account that ended up intertwining with the real checkout line. I headed to the rear of the line and waited another twenty-five minutes to finally check out. Thankfully the store took credit cards. Once outside, I spotted an ATM and withdrew Thai baht. With the shopping done, all I needed was a taxi.

By then, I was tired, hot, and thirsty. All I wanted was to be back inside my cool, air-conditioned apartment. I managed to flag down a taxi, hopped into the back, and showed him the map of my complex, hoping he would recognize it. He simply shook his head no. I kept pointing at the map, and he kept shaking his head. Finally, he pointed at the door.

"Out!" he said.

Is he seriously kicking me out?

"Out!" he shouted again.

I grabbed my bags and climbed out of the car in a huff. I stopped three more taxis. They all refused to take me to my apartment. It took another fifteen minutes for another taxi to stop. Before climbing inside, I showed him the map, and he nodded yes.

Thank God.

I climbed inside, and he drove me directly back to my building. No scenic route. No wrong drop-off point. Just a straight line from point A to point B. The fare was eighty baht, and I gave him two hundred because I was so grateful that he got me home, drama free.

When I walked into my apartment, I caught a glimpse of myself in the mirror hanging in the foyer. I looked as if I had just hiked across the Sahara Desert. Jake called just then.

"Hey, sweetie, just checking to see if you're enjoying your day."

I hung up.

Chapter Five

Client: Emily Platt
Therapist: Dr. Tammy Young
Therapy Session #: 6

Data:
Emily arrived at the session ten minutes late. She apologized profusely and explained that she lost track of time while buying party favors for Noah's one-year birthday. She tells me it's a big deal and wants everything to be perfect. She's keeping the party small and has only invited close friends and family. When asked how Jake felt about it, Emily mentioned his indifference. She couldn't understand why he felt this way and wondered out loud if Jake was genuinely threatened by an infant. She stated that Noah is also his son. When I asked why she was having a birthday party, Emily became annoyed and defended her actions with a bullet list of reasons: It was his first birthday. We're his parents. I want the memories. Emily confessed that she knows Noah's too young to enjoy the party or even remember it and that it's really a way to show him off to friends

and family. Emily described the theme she's chosen, charming San Francisco. The decor will highlight the city's sights, with Noah being the latest addition. She said she couldn't wait to dress him in his birthday outfit. It's a San Francisco Giants baseball uniform. I reminded her that during her last visit she said Noah was having trouble sleeping. She says he no longer fusses all night, and whenever she checks on him, he's sleeping soundly. I ask if she's actually seen him. She appears confused by my question and says it's strange to ask but answers yes, she sees him. During this time, Emily becomes confused and momentarily forgets what she's talking about. I reminded her that she was talking about Noah and his birthday. She remembered, and her mood changed. She's saddened and states that this Saturday would have been his first birthday.

Assessment:
Emily continues to act, think, and speak as if Noah were still alive. Emily experiences grief hallucinations: She sees and hears Noah. When in this state of mind, she also sees her husband, Jake, as the problem. However, she has moments when she knows that Noah is no longer with them. This is always accompanied by a sudden change in her behavior. The jubilant and energetic behavior she expresses quickly disappears. Jake is never mentioned as problematic during these times.

Plan:
Continue to explore Emily's two states of mind: One where Noah is alive and one where he is not. Remind Emily when she is in the latter state of mind that she has spoken and acted as if Noah were alive. Continue to explore her feelings about Jake and continue suggesting the positive role he plays in their relationship while putting forth the hypothesis that there is, in fact, no problem between Emily and her husband.

Chapter Six

Jake couldn't stop laughing when I told him about my shopping ordeal. The detail about being chased by the street dogs only made him laugh harder. At first, I was annoyed, but I eventually found the humor in it.

"This is part of the experience," he told me. "I'm sure there will be more of these types of instances. We're living in Thailand. Things are different here."

A few days later, Ploy arranged for the local telecom company to come and hook up our cable television and Wi-Fi. The plan also included a SIM card and cell service for my phone. One less daily barrier to deal with.

It was a little after four in the afternoon. The appointment for the cable provider was at 3:30. I guessed tardy cable guys were a global problem. I didn't feel like taking a walk over to the juristic office just to ask Ploy where he was. Surely she wouldn't know and would just tell me that he was on the way.

A few minutes later, there was a knock on the door, and I welcomed a smiling man in jeans and a uniform polo shirt. He smiled and gesticulated as he spoke to me in Thai. I got the impression he was apologizing for his tardiness. I nodded and smiled while pointing to the television in the living room.

It took him close to an hour to get everything set up, but we now had cable television, Wi-Fi, and, more importantly, I had a working phone. The first thing I did after the cable guy left was video call Janice, only to realize it was three in the morning her time. I did the math and realized I'd have to call her later that night around nine and catch her before she left the house for work.

The day was a bust, not that I'd had plans. I'd been doing my best to keep busy indoors by reorganizing the dishware to my liking. I know, pathetic. I still walked to the Starbucks in the morning, even though I had bought coffee for our place. Secretly, I did it because I hoped to see those women again, but I never did.

While the sun set, I took a seat on the balcony and enjoyed the warm hues in the sky. Jake had been working late every night since we arrived, usually coming home at ten or eleven. We'd have a quick chat before he'd start nodding off. I kept thinking if I had to stay home like this every day, I'd go nuts. I needed to make friends to help occupy my time.

No sooner had that thought passed through my head than I heard laughing down below. I peered over the balcony railing and spotted the three women from Starbucks I'd wanted to talk to. They were dressed in workout clothes and walking briskly on the paved pathway. If only I were out exercising, it would have been so easy to catch up and say hi.

You have time. You can catch up to them.

In a heartbeat, I had changed clothes and was out the door, running toward the elevator.

They were nowhere in sight when I got around to the other side of my building and onto the pathway. But I knew they were heading east, so I continued in that direction with hopes of finding them.

This was the first time I'd walked along the path, and I assumed it looped the property. I must have told myself at least half a dozen times since moving in that I should go for a walk and explore, but I always found a reason not to until then. As I continued, I saw no signs of the women, nor did I hear their laughter. They could have exited the pathway if they cut through a few bushes.

The sun continued to dip as I reached a part of the path that ran alongside a small pond. A Thai couple with their child had just finished feeding the ducks and were leaving. Still, I didn't see the women.

The path turned left up ahead, so anything beyond that was out of my sight. Tall banana trees eventually replaced the trimmed hedges along the route, creating a natural pergola. It was dark and quiet; by then, I'd assumed the women had left the pathway. A part of me wanted to believe they were simply walking faster than I'd realized.

Tiny lamps every few feet illuminated the pathway, but they were more decorative than anything. I stopped and contemplated turning back. Suddenly an object flew right past my face, causing me to jump back.

What the hell was that?

I spun around, thinking it was a bird, but I didn't see anything and continued walking. A second later, another object flew just above my head. And then another flapped by. These weren't birds. I screamed upon realizing that bats were flying around me. And then my biggest fear materialized. I was no longer holding Noah's hand.

"Noah!" I called out.

He had been walking alongside me not more than a few

seconds ago. How could he have disappeared from sight so quickly?

"Noah, honey. Come back to Mommy."

A bat flapped by, and I swung my hands to swat away any others.

"Noah! Where are you?"

I hurried along the pathway, frantically looking between the banana trees in case he was hiding. Sometimes Noah thinks we're playing hide and seek when we're not. I picked up the pace, assuming he'd run ahead of me.

"Noah, you need to come back to Mommy right now!"

Up ahead, the path turned another corner, and I thought Noah had run there to hide. But when I got there, I saw a dark, empty pathway ahead.

"Noah!" I continued to call out, all while my head swiveled to the left and right.

In the distance, the pathway appeared to open up, and the banana trees began to thin. I eventually popped out by the main gate at the front of the community. A security guard exited the small guard shack. Seeing him brought me back into the moment.

"Are you okay?" he asked as he approached me.

"I'm fine. I'm sorry, I got lost for a second."

He helped me around the security barrier and offered to walk me back to my building.

"I'm fine, thank you."

He smiled at me, and I noted his name tag. "Paitoon?"

"Yes," he said as he nodded enthusiastically. "Call me Pai. Easy."

"Okay, Pai. I'm Emily."

"Emily."

"Yes, that's correct.

"Okay, good night, Ms. Emily."

On the walk back to my building, I couldn't shake the heavy feeling of what had just happened. It had been three years since the therapist had deemed me recovered from the grief hallucinations I'd experienced when Noah died. As far as I and everyone around me were concerned, I was back to normal, my sane self. And yet, I had been convinced that Noah was with me only a few minutes ago. I hoped the sightings weren't coming back. It would ruin everything.

Chapter Seven

OVER THE NEXT FEW DAYS, I remained in the apartment, venturing once to pick up some items from the nearby 7-Eleven. I didn't dare tell Jake about what had happened that evening on the pathway. I knew he would want me to, but with him working so hard to get his footing in his new position, the last thing I wanted was to be a distraction for him.

Those first two years after Noah's death were devastating and troubling for me, but they were equally hard for Jake. Not only was he grieving his lost son, but he also had to deal with me.

"I've lost my son; I can't bear to lose you, too," he'd told me one night while we laid in bed.

Jake had been true to his word. He stuck by me during the most challenging time of our relationship. I know it wasn't easy for him, and it tested his patience, but he did not make me feel bad or guilty about my condition. Eventually, we made it through. My therapist, Dr. Tammy Young, was a godsend. She was instrumental in helping me work through my grief.

Did I have a relapse? Should I reach out to Dr. Young? Or is this just stress?

I decided to push through on my own, chalking that episode up to stress. I was still trying to settle into my new life in Thailand, and I needed to cut myself some slack.

But I also realized I couldn't stay indoors forever.

An idle mind is the devil's workshop.

I changed into shorts and a blouse and forced myself to walk to Starbucks for a coffee, even though I wasn't in the mood. I passed Pai on the way.

"Ms. Emily. Hello," he said with a wave.

"Hello, Pai."

His was the only friendly smile I'd seen in days. The previous two nights, Jake had come home after I was in bed and was off to work before I woke. It was the weekend, but he'd already warned me that weekends in the office would be a given for the time being. In fact, we hadn't even been able to have dinner together to celebrate our arrival in Thailand. But I understood. Jake was the new guy and needed to prove himself. It was my turn to be patient and stand by his side. It would get better.

Chatting with Janice should have been a lifesaver, but I couldn't just pick up the phone and call her like I usually would because of the different time zones. I had to plan my calls, and even then, I would catch her in the morning when she was hurrying to get ready for work, or late at night when she was tired. Don't get me wrong, Janice did her best to keep the conversations going. She called, but it wasn't the same. The time difference was incredibly inconvenient for both of us.

I walked with my head down, my eyes trained on the sidewalk, watching my steps as I closed in on the Starbucks. Suddenly, I ran into someone, and I looked up quickly.

"I'm so sorry," I blurted.

"Quite all right," the woman said.

It took a second for me to recognize her. She was one of the women I'd been trying to chase down ever since my first visit to the coffee shop. She looked to be in her early forties and had that same confident look on her face I'd noticed the first time I saw her, with her left brow arched. She was dressed sharply, in a skirt suit with a Chanel purse hanging off her shoulder. Her dirty blonde hair sat in a cute, tousled bob.

"You speak English," I said, only to regret saying it as soon as the words left my mouth.

"Yes, last time I checked," she said. "It's Emily, right?"

"Oh, uh, yes, that's right. How did you know?"

"I believe our husbands work together."

"I'm sorry. I haven't had a chance to meet any of Jake's colleagues. Jake's my husband. What's your husband's name?"

"It's Kip Wagner. He's the managing director of the Southeast Asia region." She stuck her hand out. "I'm Vivian Wagner."

"It's so nice to meet you."

"Listen, I'm in a hurry right now. I have an appointment, but if you're not busy, why don't you join me here tomorrow morning at eight. I'll introduce you to the others."

"I'm free! I mean, that sounds great. I'll be here at eight."

"Sharp." Vivian tapped at her wristwatch with a smile before walking off.

Way to go, eager beaver. Can you be any more desperate for friendship?

I might have come across like the new kid in school who was tired of sitting alone in the cafeteria, but I didn't care. I had just made my first friend, and I was thrilled.

For the remainder of the day and night, I must have tried on every outfit I had, wanting to make the perfect impression with Vivian and the other two women. I wasn't sure if she was just being nice because our husbands worked together or if she was genuinely interested in being friends with me. I didn't care; I needed to talk to someone besides myself.

When Jake came home, I was in our bedroom, standing in front of a mirror, dressed in an outfit I had tried on earlier. He cleared his throat as he stood in the doorway. "Looks like a tornado came through here."

Clothes were spread out over the bed, and there must have been about twenty pairs of shoes scattered across the carpeting.

"Sorry about the mess," I said as I kissed him.

"I'm glad I don't have this problem. I'd never make it to work."

"I'm trying to decide what to wear tomorrow. I've narrowed my selection down to three outfits."

"What's going on tomorrow?"

"I made a friend, or I think I did."

"That's great."

"Her name's Vivian, and she said her husband works with you. Does the name Kip ring a bell?"

"Kip Wagner? He's my boss."

"Oh, well, no wonder she knew who I was. Um, will that be a problem for you?"

Jake shook his head. "I don't see it being one. Kip and I get along well."

"Good, because I'm set to meet her tomorrow at eight, and she's going to introduce me to a few other women. I'm assuming they're also expats. Maybe their husbands also work at your company."

"Maybe, there are a lot of foreigners employed there."

Jake eyed the clothes on the bed. "Did you need help deciding?"

I smiled. He knew me so well. I modeled the three outfits, and Jake said his favorite was the white dress.

"It'll be hot, and that dress will keep you cool. Forget the jeans."

"You're right. I think the dress is the right choice."

Jake wrapped his arms around me. "Plus, you look incredibly sexy in it. I want everyone to know I got the hottest wife around here."

"I promise I won't let you down."

Chapter Eight

I WAS UP EARLY the following morning and was able to see Jake off to work. It was only a ten-minute walk to the Starbucks, but I didn't want anything to go wrong. So I showered, got dressed, and then waited until 7:45, at which time I left my apartment. I had it planned perfectly so that I would arrive at five minutes to eight. Not obnoxiously early, but enough to signal that I was responsible. But when I arrived, I was surprised to see all three women sitting around the table with coffees already in their hands. Vivian was in the middle of telling an engaging story.

I glanced at my watch quickly, thinking maybe I had misjudged my arrival time, but I hadn't. I then thought I might have gotten the time mixed up. I was sure Vivian had said eight sharp, but it looked as if they had all arrived much earlier.

"Emily, how nice of you to join us," Vivian said, flashing a quick smile.

"I'm sorry I'm late."

"That's fine. I'm sure it won't happen again."

Again? But I wasn't really late.

"Emily, I'd like to introduce you to Jackie and Kimmy. Ladies, this is Emily, the woman I told you about earlier."

"It's nice to meet you," Jackie said as she extended a hand.

"Same here," said Kimmy. "Welcome to Thailand."

I shook both of their hands before excusing myself to get a coffee. When I returned, I sat in the one empty chair. There was only enough room around the table for four chairs, so I was glad I didn't have to squeeze in and make the situation any more awkward. I still believed I'd had the time right.

"So, where do you hail from?" Jackie asked as I settled in.

"I'm from San Francisco. I grew up there. This is my first time in Thailand—or Southeast Asia, for that matter. How long have you all been here?"

"Kimmy and I have been here for two years. I think we arrived within a week of each other." Kimmy nodded in agreement. "But Vivian's been here much longer."

"Oh?" I looked at Vivian, expecting her to chime in, but she just sat there smiling as she eyed me.

Jackie and Kimmy were both wearing gigantic rocks on their left ring fingers, so I assumed they were married.

"Do your husbands also work at Asia Pacific Holdings?"

"Don't they all?" Jackie said, laughing.

"She's kidding," Kimmy said. "There are several large international firms in Thailand. A lot of people seem to be employed in the petroleum industry."

We continued with the getting-to-know-each-other conversation, and I learned a lot about Jackie and Kimmy. Both seemed friendly and welcoming, but Vivian remained quiet during the conversation, which I found strange. Whenever I'd seen them in the past, she had appeared to be the one speaking and holding the attention of the others. So why was she suddenly quiet?

Did she change her mind about me?

Was she not the leader of the group?

Or was she simply deciding if I was worthy or not?

If I had to put my money on one of the three, it would be the last. Vivian hadn't stopped eyeing me from the moment I sat down. It was so bad that I had difficulty maintaining eye contact with her. Even with her being silent, her presence across the table intimidated me with the way her gaze locked onto me, one brow arched sharply as her smile curved up higher on the same side.

Are you analyzing me, Vivian?

I decided not to make snap judgments. I liked Vivian, even if it did seem like she was evaluating me for flaws. I definitely saw myself being friends with Jackie and Kimmy. Both were warm and inviting.

"How are you getting along so far?" Kimmy asked.

"Well, grocery shopping turned into an ordeal," I said. I quickly recounted the story for them, which had them in stitches.

"You poor thing," Kimmy said. "First off, don't shop at Big C. You're much better off at Villa Market. They have a large selection of imports to satisfy your cravings from home."

"Where is Villa Market?"

"It's much farther away, but the shuttle will drop you off and pick you up."

"What shuttle?"

"The complimentary shuttle service for our complex. It will drop you off at the BTS Skytrain station and Villa Market."

"Or you can hire a driver," Vivian added.

"Yes, most of the time, that's what we do," Jackie said. "But occasionally, I'll hop on the shuttle bus. I don't mind it."

Kimmy quickly ran down the schedule, the drop-off and pick-up points and times, and assessed each driver. There were three of them.

They then told me the best places to get my nails and hair

done, what spas were top-notch and which were alleyway quality at best. They also ran down a list of their favorite places to shop and dine.

"We absolutely love having lunch there," Jackie said as she got through describing a downtown bistro. "You'll have to join us."

"I'd like that—it sounds fun," I said. "You guys are a wealth of information. I can't thank you enough. I've felt so lost since coming here. Even the simplest of tasks seems extraordinary."

"Don't worry; it gets easier," Jackie said. "Stick with us, and you'll be a veteran expat in no time."

"Absolutely, and we'll teach you all the secret shortcuts to getting stuff done here," Kimmy said.

"Shortcuts?" I asked as I crinkled my brow.

Vivian cleared her throat. "This town revolves around who you keep company with," she said. "Who you know can make things easy, or it can make them impossible. Remember that."

My initial impression was that Jackie was the mother of the group: caring, consoling, and definitely a shoulder to cry on. Kimmy was absolutely the organizer/information go-to. And Vivian—I still pegged her as the leader, even though she kept her cards close. She was the one who made the first move and invited me to join them. I didn't really see the other two doing that. Plus, they constantly glanced at her as if they were seeking approval, especially if they were doling out information.

So where did that leave me? If I were being accepted into this friend group, was I the newbie? I was okay with that so long as I didn't become the punching bag, but I expected that I might get a little of that while I found my footing. It would be very much like things were for Jake at work. I'd be proving myself initially, but eventually, I should be able to fall into my place in the group. In my head, I was the trustworthy friend that they all could count on. I'd be grounded and definitely neutral if it came to picking sides.

"Have you guys decided what you're wearing tonight?" Kimmy asked. "I still can't decide."

"What do you mean?" Jackie asked. "I thought you were wearing the black dress."

"I am. I just can't decide between sleeves or no sleeves."

"Go sleeveless," Jackie said before turning to me. "What are you wearing, Emily?"

"Uh, um..."

"You're coming, right?"

"I'm sorry. What is it we're talking about?"

"Tonight, there's a fashion gala," Vivian said. "Everyone who's anyone will be there. You have to be there if you're with us."

"I, um... Yes, sure. I'd love to attend."

"Great. Now that that's settled, I have a hair appointment."

"Oh, me too. I want to get my color touched up," Kimmy said.

"I'll come with you," Jackie said.

"Where's the gala at, and what time is it?" I blurted out.

"Six-thirty sharp, at the top of Iconsiam," Vivian said as she walked away. "And please dress to impress," she said, eyeing me one last time.

Within seconds all three women had taken off, leaving me sitting at the table alone and wondering if I was invited. It dawned on me that I'd forgotten to exchange contact information with the others. Heck, I didn't even know what Iconsiam was. I quickly Googled it, and found out it was a luxury shopping center known for hosting glamorous events. In the "upcoming events" section, a fashion gala was scheduled for later that evening.

I hurried home and tried to decide if I had something appropriate to wear to a fashion gala, or if I needed to quickly run out and buy something. Vivian said to dress appropriately. The only problem was I'd never attended a fashion gala.

Chapter Nine

I chose an elegant black dress with a single strand of pearls and matching earrings. Jake thought I looked great. I felt a little guilty, because of all the nights he could have come home early, that was the night he did.

"I'm sorry," I said.

"Don't be. Go out. Have fun. Me, I got a date with the couch over there. And if I'm not mistaken, there's a block of cheese in the fridge and a stick of salami on the counter. I'm set for the night."

Jake was already changing into an old pair of sweats. There was no hiding his enthusiasm to remain at home with his cheese.

And I was so glad I did attend the event (and in the dress I chose), as it turned out to be black-tie. Iconsiam was more than a high-end shopping mall; it was something I'd never seen before. I wouldn't even call it a mall. It was more like a destination venue for the rich. The entire place was filled with luxury brands and designer boutiques. It smelled of hi-so money. During my research, I had learned that there were two significant classifications for people in Bangkok: hi-so, short for high society folks, and low-so, short for the less wealthy.

The event was being held on the top floors of the mall, which apparently were built to hold conventions. I took the numerous escalators up to the top floor, where two smiling men in suits greeted me. They wanted to see my invitation, which was a problem because I didn't have one. Vivian and the others didn't tell me I would need to show one.

"I was invited by Vivian Wagner. Is there a guest list that can be checked?"

The two men did nothing but stare back at me. It just so happened I noticed Jackie passing behind them.

"Jackie!" I shouted, waving my arm.

She turned, and a smile formed on her face. "Emily. So glad you made it." She hurried over.

Jackie didn't say a single word to the men, but as soon as they saw her, they promptly stepped off to the side and motioned for me to pass. No questions asked.

"Follow me. We're in the back."

"I'm so glad I saw you," I said. "I didn't have an invite, and it didn't look like those men were letting me in."

"Well, it's a good thing I had to go to the restroom. You might have been waiting out here all night."

We walked past what appeared to be a runway, which I assumed would be used later in the evening. Vivian and the others were standing in a group near the bar. And from the looks of it, they'd all brought their husbands.

No one mentioned we could bring our husbands.

"Ladies, look who I found on the way back from the restroom," Jackie announced.

"Emily, so happy to see you," Kimmy said.

"Emily dear, you look fabulous," Vivian said, which, I admit, felt extra special coming from her.

"But where's Jake? Why didn't you bring him?" She looked beyond me.

"I didn't know I could; I wasn't told we could bring our husbands."

"Oh, don't be silly. I told you to bring him."

"Yeah, then he could have stood around feeling out of place like the rest of us," the man standing next to Vivian said. "I'm Kip. Vivian's other half."

"It's nice to finally meet you. I've heard Jake mention your name. All good things, of course."

"Glad to hear it. He's doing a great job, and I'm happy to have him as part of the team."

I met Jackie's husband, Ned, and Kimmy's husband, Garret, who were both pleasant. I wished Jake was there for me to show off, but I knew he was happy at home with his cheese.

Over the next thirty minutes, I followed Vivian and the others as they worked the room. They knew everyone there, and the few individuals they didn't know were happy to have met them. And the best part was that Vivian personally introduced me to every single person they spoke with.

"This is Emily; she's with us," she would say.

Those six magical words changed everything. It was as if I'd been suddenly elevated to godlike status. People tripped over themselves to meet me while bombarding me with questions. The attention was unlike anything I'd ever experienced. To say I felt special was an understatement. I felt like royalty. And the invites? Everyone had something to invite me to, whether it was another gala or the grand opening of a boutique, or even to have dinner at their restaurant. And it wasn't just other expats I was being introduced to; most of the attendees were hi-so Thais. Even the Thai elite showed up. They were the powerful family dynasties that went way back.

All I could do to keep up was nod and say "Thank you." During one of those exchanges, I glanced at Vivian and caught her staring at me. Instead of a smile on her face, there was a look that sent a shiver through my body. A second later, she smiled, hooked her arm around mine, and led me to the next power couple on her list of people to know.

Whatever apprehensions I might have harbored about Vivian had disappeared by the time the fashion show started. She had done nothing but make sure everyone there knew I was a bona fide member of their friend group.

And the photographs—I must have more than a hundred snapped of me. Photographers at the event wanted pictures of me with everyone I spoke to. I even posed with the fashion models and designers after the runway show. I was convinced they had mistaken me for someone else.

Vivian told me to keep smiling. "Think of this as your inauguration."

"But I'm no one."

"You're with me. You're someone."

As soon as I had a chance, I broke away and ran to the restroom. I thought I was going to explode. On the way out, I bumped into a woman I'd been introduced to earlier. Her name was Meredith Brown. She was from Australia and a mother of two. Her husband was a high-level executive in the petroleum industry.

"Are you having fun tonight?" she asked.

"It's been incredible. Everyone here is so nice and inviting."

"Well, you're with Vivian now. Expect more of that. Many others have tried to grab that spot you have, but all have failed."

"Spot?"

"The fourth spot in the friend group. It's been vacant for a while."

"Wait, are you saying there's a cap on how many friends are in the group?"

"You didn't hear it from me, but from what I know, Vivian likes to keep the group small. I mean, I totally get it. The attention and privilege afforded to the group, especially in the Thai community, doesn't come easy. You should be proud to have been chosen."

"Um, yeah. Vivian, Jackie, and Kimmy have been nothing but nice and helpful in getting me acclimated to the Bangkok scene."

"I wish I had that when I first arrived. It can be difficult. I'd say it's worth putting up with all those rules."

"What rules?" I did a double-take at Meredith.

She smiled. "I know you're not supposed to discuss them outside of your group. Don't worry. I'll keep my mouth shut." Meredith made a zipper movement across her lips.

"No, wait. What do you mean by 'rules'?"

Meredith crinkled her brow. "Don't you know? There are rules Vivian expects members of the group to follow. I heard you're allowed to break a rule once. After that, it's adios amigos."

"Are you sure? That doesn't sound right. I've never heard them mention anything about rules, nor would I expect them to. Are you sure you're talking about the right people?"

Meredith smiled. "I wouldn't worry too much about it. You seem to be doing just fine." Meredith gave me a once-over. "You're dressed appropriately. No need to worry about that rule. It's been nice talking to you. We'll catch up later. I need to get my husband away from that bar. He's getting too cozy."

I thought about what Meredith had said...the rules. And I wondered what other rules there were besides dressing right.

Chapter Ten

When I woke up Saturday morning, I slid my arm over to Jake's side of the bed and felt emptiness. I assumed he'd headed into the office. He had been asleep when I came home the night before. I remembered checking the fridge out of curiosity and seeing that he'd eaten three-quarters of a block of cheddar and half a salami stick. I'd always admired Jake's ability to eat anything, and it have no effect on his physique. On the other hand, I just needed to glance at a slice of cake, and the pounds materialized.

I forced myself out of bed and stopped in the bathroom before heading out into the living room. To my surprise, Jake was sitting on the couch drinking coffee.

"Good morning, sleepyhead," he said.

"Good morning," I said as I hurried over to him and snuggled up into his side. "Why didn't you wake me?"

"You looked like you were enjoying your sleep."

"Are you not working today?"

"Nope. I'm free."

I took his mug from him and took a sip of his coffee.

"How was your fashion gala last night?" he asked.

"Where do I start?"

There was so much to tell Jake that I fixed my own cup of coffee for the energy it would take to get through it all.

"First off, you could have totally come to the gala," I said as I sat back down. "All the husbands were there. I met your boss, Kip."

"Kip was there?"

"Yeah, but I swear no one told me I could bring you—or should. I'm sorry."

"Don't worry about it. I was happier at home. And I'm sure Kip hated every minute there."

"Well, he did crack a joke about being dragged there."

"Yeah, it's fine. So, other than me missing out on watching skinny women walk down the catwalk in weird-looking dresses, what else happened?"

I went on to tell Jake about all the people Vivian introduced to me. "Not only did I meet a ton of other expats, but I also met so many Thai people. And I'm talking, like, the high-society Thai. You should have seen the jewels on these women."

"Wow, that's incredible. Soon you'll be one of the most connected people in Bangkok."

"That's right, and I'll be able to get us the best tables at the best restaurants if I can get over my imposter syndrome. I felt like a fish out of water."

"You'll get used to it."

I went on to tell him about all the invitations to dinner parties and luncheons I'd received. "Also, it seems like everyone here is opening some sort of business and throwing a party to announce it. I was invited to four different grand openings in one week alone. But I suspect many of them are pet projects. Apparently, it's something the wealthy here do with their money."

"Sounds like it."

"Oh, I almost forgot. I met a woman named Meredith Brown. Does that name sound familiar to you?"

Jake shook his head no.

"She's an Australian. Her husband works for one of the petroleum companies. Anyway, you know what she told me?"

"What?"

"That there are rules in my friend group."

"You mean with Vivian and the others?"

"Yes. Apparently, being friends with them is, like, a big deal. It's why so many people were eager to meet and take photos with me. I'm sure I would have had a much different experience last night if I wasn't with them."

"Aw, come on. They can't be that important."

"Oh yes, they are. In fact, I wouldn't have gotten into the gala if it wasn't for Jackie. Anyway, I'm getting off track. Back to this Meredith woman and the rules. She told me Vivian has rules for people in the group to follow, meaning me, Jackie, and Kimmy."

"What are the rules?"

"Well, she didn't outright list them; she just mentioned that I was dressed appropriately and that looking good was a rule. She was surprised that I didn't know, like it was common knowledge."

"That sounds dumb. Who makes their friends follow rules?"

"That's what I was thinking. Vivian, Jackie, and Kimmy have been nothing but nice to me. I really see us developing a tight friendship. Plus, Vivian went out of her way to introduce me to everyone there and made it clear that I was with her, which ties back to her being well-connected in Bangkok. I'm guessing you working with Kip is also a plus."

Jake shrugged. "I guess. Are you sure you're not just reading into this?"

"No. Because I met another woman later that night, Kathy

something. I couldn't understand what she said because she'd had a lot to drink and was slurring, but I'm positive she mentioned the rules. She said, and I quote, 'Do the rules bother you?'"

"She asked that?"

"I shit you not."

"Did she bother to list them out?"

"No, that's the thing; they don't even want to be caught talking about it. She lowered her voice and leaned in when she said it."

"This sounds like a lot of catty talk. These women are probably jealous that you just got here, and now you're friends with Vivian."

"I was thinking the same thing. Meredith mentioned that Vivian keeps the group small, just four women, so it makes sense that my spot is coveted."

"You're a perfect addition. Who wouldn't want to be friends with you? Don't overthink it. It's not worth it."

"You're right. But it's just weird that these women would say it."

"Dressing right doesn't really sound like a rule to me. It's more like common sense. I thought you picked the right outfit for last night. It's a no-brainer."

"Now that I think about it, Kathy—I wish I could remember her last name—did mention another rule about not discussing anything outside the group."

"Okay, so keeping things within your group sounds normal. Like it's an unwritten rule that what you guys discuss with each other is for your ears only. Kind of like what we discuss. I think these women are jealous and are trying to mine you for information or, at the very least, figure out how you got into the group. Just watch what you say to people."

"You're right."

Jake put his arm around me and pulled me closer. "Do you have plans today?"

"No, I don't. We can do something together."

"I know exactly what we can do together." Jake flashed me his devious smile before scooping me up in his arms and carrying me back to the bedroom.

Chapter Eleven

AFTER OUR MORNING SEXATHON, Jake wanted to get something to eat. While he showered, I checked my phone and saw that I'd received a text message from Vivian. The group was meeting for lunch at noon, and she hoped I hadn't forgotten, as the reservations were highly coveted. It was 10:30.

Had we made plans? I couldn't remember. The night before had been a whirlwind, but I might have agreed to meet them.

"What's wrong?" Jake asked as he exited the bathroom.

"I just got a message from Vivian about a luncheon I had agreed to attend. I don't remember it."

"Go have fun. I'll be fine. I'll order a pizza."

"Are you sure?"

"Yeah, totally. We'll hang out tonight."

"It's just that we haven't had much time together since we moved to Thailand. I don't want you to feel like I'm blowing you off."

"I don't. Look, I've already opened the app for delivery. I'm good. Trust me. I'll see you after. I'll be right there." He pointed at the couch.

I jumped into the shower and then got ready as quickly as

possible, knowing I wanted to be there just a little early in case Vivian meant to say 11:30 instead of noon. I booked a taxi on a ride-sharing app, but not a car, because traffic would be hell. I opted for a motorbike. Sure, my hair might get tossed, but I wouldn't be late. And that's what was important to me.

My driver sped between cars and even up on the sidewalk at times just to keep moving forward through the stop-and-go traffic. I was grateful for his aggressive driving as we got to the restaurant with minutes to spare. I hurried over to the restaurant while raking my hand through my hair.

"Hi, I'm meeting friends for lunch," I said to the hostess. "I can just look for them alone if that's fine."

"Is there a name?"

"Um, maybe. If there is, it's probably under Vivian Wagner."

"Oh, Mrs. Wagner. Yes, she has a reservation, but she hasn't arrived yet. I can seat you if you wish?"

"That would be great."

I couldn't believe I had arrived first. I took my seat and waited with a patient smile. I busied myself on my phone, glancing up every few seconds to see if anyone had arrived. I didn't think much about their tardiness until fifteen minutes had passed without a peep.

Hmmm, that's strange. Surely, they can't all be running late.

I rechecked the message Vivian had sent just to make sure I had read the time and restaurant correctly. I had.

The restaurant was packed and full of lively discussions, mostly groups of women. I did spy a couple of tables with older men sitting with young women. And they weren't their daughters.

At 12:30, I started to wonder if something was wrong. It wasn't like any of them to be thirty minutes late. Plus, there weren't any new messages in the group chat. I was about to fire off a message when I saw them walk into the restaurant, laughing, as Vivian appeared to be telling yet another story.

I won't lie. I was a bit irritated. I'd busted my hump to get to the restaurant on time, only to watch them casually walk in thirty minutes late. And they didn't seem at all bothered by that.

"Emily, how are you?" Vivian said as she took a seat. "We were just talking about the gala last night. Wasn't it so much fun?"

"Uh, yeah, I had a great time."

Jackie gave me a hug before taking a seat next to me. She was the hugger in the group. And I really appreciated that hug right then.

"Everyone was so pleased to meet you last night," Vivian continued. "You made quite the impression."

"Really?"

"Oh, yes," Kimmy said. "I heard the same. Everyone loved you."

"Wow, I'm not sure what to say to that."

"Say nothing," Jackie said. "Bask in it. That's all you need to do."

We talked more about the previous night's gala before the topic switched to the school where Jackie and Kimmy sent their children. Jackie had two boys. Kimmy had a boy and a girl. Vivian didn't have kids, as far as I knew. She was definitely the oldest one in the group. She never mentioned her age. It was possible that she did have kids when she was really young, and they were grown and out of the house by now. I didn't feel comfortable enough to ask.

"I can't believe they're raising the tuition," Jackie said.

Apparently, the school their children attended cost a fortune. It was the most prestigious international school in Bangkok. Jackie and Kimmy weren't sure if the company would raise the school allowance they received as part of their expat package.

"I'm sure the company will give you more money," Vivian said. "It's the right thing to do."

"I hope so," Kimmy said.

"I'll talk to Kip and see if he has any sway," Vivian offered.

It turned out that Jackie's and Kimmy's husbands also reported to Kip. I wondered briefly if that was why we were all friends. Probably helped. There was an instant commonality.

Lunch was delicious. These women certainly did know how to dine. And Vivian picked up the tab, even with us protesting to pay our shares. But she insisted we could split the bill the next time around.

"Emily, do you have plans today?" Jackie asked.

"Um, not really."

"Great. You're coming shopping with us," Vivian said.

"Oh, uh, okay. Where are we going?"

"I think the question is, 'Where are we not going?'" Kimmy said. "And also, I'm hosting a mimosa get-together at my place on Sunday morning. I expect all of you to be there."

"Ooh, mimosas. I'll be there," Jackie said.

"Count me in," said Vivian.

At that point, all eyes turned toward me. "Who doesn't like mimosas? I'll be there."

In my head, I thought I could still spend some quality time with Jake on Saturday night and whatever could be salvaged from Sunday. Even though I was sure we were all friends by that point, this nagging bit of my brain made me feel as if I were still on some sort of probation. Maybe this was because I didn't have the history or the bond that Vivian and the others did. But I had to start somewhere.

"Are we inviting our husbands?" I asked, just to be sure the same thing that had happened at the gala didn't happen here.

"Boss bitches only," Jackie said, lifting her glass. The others raised their glasses, as did I. "No one else need apply."

"Come on, ladies," Vivian said as she stood. "The stores are calling our names."

We ended up at a nearby shopping center that specialized in luxury brands. Vivian went crazy inside the Chanel store, snapping up a handbag, a pair of shoes, sunglasses, and a dress. Jackie and Kimmy each bought purses. I also saw one that I absolutely loved. But the price tag had me doing a double take. And even though Jake had more than doubled his salary by taking this job, I was used to buying something at this price only after debating it for weeks.

"Come on, Emily. Get it." Jackie said. "Jake will love it on you."

"Model it for him in the nude," Kimmy said. "You'll hear no complaints."

Before I knew it, I had laid down my credit card and was the new owner of a Chanel purse.

After we left the Chanel store, I excused myself and went to the ladies' room. On my way out, I ran into Meredith, the Australian woman I had met at the fashion gala.

"Emily, so good to see you again," she said. A little girl stood by her side.

"Hi, Meredith. And who's this little one?"

"This is my daughter, Susie. Say hi, Susie."

The little girl flashed a quick smile with a wave before hiding behind Meredith's leg.

I reached down behind my leg to introduce Noah, but couldn't feel him. I looked behind me before spinning around.

"Did you lose something?" Meredith asked.

"I uh, um..."

I suddenly snapped back into the present and realized what had happened.

"I'm sorry. I'm just a little scatterbrained today," I said, looking at Susie, who was peeking out from behind Meredith's leg.

"Are you here shopping?" she asked, eyeing my bag.

"I met Vivian and the others for lunch, and of course, there's some shopping."

"I love coming to this shopping center. It's lovely, isn't it?"

"Better than the ones we have back in the States. Plus, the restaurants here are amazing, but I'll admit they are pricey."

"It adds up."

"Tomorrow, we're all heading to Kimmy's place for mimosas, so that'll help," I said.

"Oh, that sounds nice."

"What? You have a confused look on your face," I said.

"It's just that...oh, never mind."

"What? You can't say that and then suddenly clam up."

"I was under the impression..." Meredith looked around and then spoke in a much softer voice. "I thought it was against one of the rules. You know, sharing what's discussed in the group."

Meredith's comment caught me off guard. "Uh, I think it's fine to mention that. I don't see the big deal."

"Hey, if it's fine with you, it's fine with me. You're just lucky to be part of the group. Also, eating and shopping only at approved locations is a small price to pay for the amazing perks that being a part of that friend group affords you."

"Approved locations? I think these rule rumors are getting out of control," I said with a chuckle.

Meredith shrugged. "You would know. Maybe Vivian's relaxed them."

Susie whined just then. "Mommy, I have to go pee-pee."

"Duty calls," Meredith said. "See you around."

"See you."

As I walked away from the bathrooms, I spotted Vivian in the distance, watching me.

"Was that Meredith Brown I saw you talking to?" she asked as I approached her.

"Yes, I ran into her on the way out. Do you know her well?"

"I know her well enough. She's a bit of a gossiper. Be careful of what you say around her. Once you tell her something, she becomes the town crier."

"Oh, okay. Good to know. She did mention something that sounded weird. In fact, she's mentioned it both times I've run into her...something about rules in our friend group."

"That's just Meredith being nosy. Every group of friends has its unwritten rules, like having each other's backs, and private things we discuss stay between us. She's just trying to make it a bigger deal than it is. Normal stuff."

"Well, when you put it that way, it makes sense."

"You know, Meredith tried to be a part of our group."

"Oh? What happened?"

"She's nice, but she just didn't vibe with us. It was nothing like you. We all vibed the minute we met. Don't you agree?"

"Yes, of course."

"That's life. We can't all be best friends with everyone. Come on, Jackie and Kimmy are waiting for us."

Chapter Twelve

Client: Emily Platt
Therapist: Dr. Tammy Young
Therapy session #: 15

Data:
Emily showed up in a happy mood, so I asked about her day. She responded that she and Jake had spent the weekend in Napa Valley. They drank a lot of wine and had a relaxing weekend. She admitted that they needed that reconnection. She made it a point to say that the sex was better than usual. I asked her what she thought made it better this time than in the past. Emily believes it was just getting out of the city and spending quality time together. Also, they spent the weekend at the same hotel where she thinks they were staying when she first got pregnant. She crossed her fingers and smiled. When asked if they were trying to get pregnant, she stated it wasn't the case, but Noah wasn't planned either. She thinks she might be ready to try again but isn't sure after losing Noah. She states she has good and bad days but feels like she's making progress and coping

better with her loss now than in the past. I asked if she still kept Noah's room the same way. She admitted to boxing up his things, but that they weren't planning on throwing any of it away. Emily mentioned that it helped to not see the crib in Noah's room. It only reminded her of what could have been. I asked how Jake was, and she said he was great and she loved being married to him. She still hasn't openly acknowledged that Jake is also grieving the loss of their son. Whenever I bring it up, she deflects or quickly changes the subject.

Assessment:
Emily shows signs of coping with her grief. She no longer appears to be experiencing grief hallucinations and speaks about Noah in the past tense. She doesn't recall complaining about Jake, which leads me to believe those thoughts and accusations only existed in her previous state of mind. There could be a divide between her and Jake. It's important that she realize that they both lost a child, and not only her. There is concern that she is falling into a reality where only she exists.

Plan:
Continue working with Emily on overcoming her grief. Encourage her to continue spending quality time with Jake, as he is also grieving. It's vital that they both recognize each other's feelings and loss. Especially Emily.

Chapter Thirteen

IT WAS after 8:00 p.m. when I returned home. I couldn't wait to change out of my outfit into something much better suited for snuggling with my husband. Jake had picked up two bottles of wine, and we planned to spend the entire evening on the sofa while binging something on Netflix.

"I'm so sorry about today," I said as I sat.

"Don't worry about it. We're good now." He slipped an arm around me and pulled me into him.

"What did you do today?" I asked.

"I lounged around, ate pizza, and watched TV. It was perfect."

"Perfect without me?"

"Almost," he chuckled. "How was lunch with the girls?"

"The restaurant where we ate was so good. They have this amazing penne alla vodka. I absolutely loved it."

"Sounds good. I'll have to try these amazing places you're eating at."

"You must. These restaurants are amazing. And get this, everyone knows Vivian. Today I arrived early, and the others weren't there yet. I swear the hostess wasn't giving me the time

The Friend Group

of day until I told her I was meeting Vivian Wagner." I snapped my fingers. "Just like that, she became very attentive, showing me to a perfect table toward the back of the restaurant that allowed me a view of everyone there. But I was a little annoyed because I busted my hump to get to the restaurant on time, and they showed up thirty minutes late. And before you say maybe I got the time wrong, I didn't. I checked the message Vivian sent, and it said noon sharp."

"Meh, it's not that big of a deal."

"I know, but it's just weird that she comes across as a stickler for punctuality until it applies to her."

"Are the other two like that, Jackie and Kimmy?"

"Not really. I mean, they're really easy. They just go with the flow. Vivian is the one who's a stickler for—"

"The rules?"

"Yes! That's right."

"It's probably just her personality. She might have OCD, like Monica from that TV show *Friends*."

"I guess. I never thought of it that way."

"She likes order and things to be a certain way."

"Definitely."

"Does it bother you?"

"Um, good question. It really shouldn't, because she really is nice. I can see that she means well. She always wants to pay, and she's never once made me feel like an outsider to the group. She's gone above and beyond trying to make me feel included in everything, and she's made sure others outside the group know that as well."

"So what's the problem? She seems like someone you want in your corner, especially with her connections in town."

"It's these rules, or supposed rules, I keep hearing about. Today I ran into Meredith outside the restroom."

"That's the woman from Australia, right?"

"Yes. Anyway, she asked how I was and what I was up to, so I told her I had just finished eating lunch with Vivian, Jackie, and Kimmy and that we were shopping. I also mentioned that we were having a brunch get-together at Kimmy's tomorrow, and she was shocked that I had divulged that. She thought it was against the 'rules.'"

"She actually said that?"

"Yes, Jake. I swear I'm not exaggerating."

"I still think these are just basic unwritten friendship rules," Jake said, yawning. "You know, like the understanding we have about our private conversations. It's not like we need to draft bylaws and pin them on the fridge."

"I know, I know."

"I bet it's just this woman who's blowing it out of proportion."

"Could be. Vivian saw me talking to Meredith. I asked if she knew her, and she said she knew her enough to know Meredith loved to gossip. She said to be careful of what I say around her."

"You see, that's completely normal. Nobody wants their dirty laundry aired."

"That's kind of how Vivian portrayed it. Oh, get this. Vivian said Meredith at one point wanted to be a part of the group, but Vivian said she and the others just didn't vibe all that well with Meredith."

"That's it. She's bitter and doesn't want anyone else to join the group. Just forget about it. It's nothing." Jake looked off to the side at the Chanel shopping bag I had brought home. "I'm guessing eating wasn't the only thing you did."

"No, but before you say anything, I just want you to know it's an amazing purse, and I'll get so much use out of it. Plus, the quality is top-notch."

"Yeah? Let me see this amazing bag."

I hopped up and fetched the bag. "Wait one minute." I ran

into the bedroom, stripped off all my clothes, slipped on black heels, and then came back.

"I present Chanel's classic black handbag made with grained calfskin."

I spun around with the purse hanging off my shoulder.

"Perfect for an evening out."

I sashayed over to Jake and placed a heel on the sofa next to his crotch. "Or a casual stroll in the park."

"More like a romp in the park," said Jake, laughing.

"It would go well with that, too," I said with a smile. "Care to take it for a spin?"

"I think I'll need to if I'm to give this bag my stamp of approval."

Chapter Fourteen

THE FOLLOWING MORNING, I woke early. Jake was still in a deep sleep, so I didn't bother him. I fixed myself a cup of coffee and sat out on the balcony. It was peaceful, quiet, and, most importantly, still cool.

I'm not sure what triggered it, but I started thinking about the stupid rules Meredith had mentioned. Every part of me said to give it up and not waste more time thinking about it. And I was prepared to do that, right after I did one other thing.

This wasn't the first friend group that I had been a part of. I'd been in numerous friend groups, and there were commonalities. I grabbed my tablet and started making a list of the supposed rules I had heard through the rumor mill over the last few weeks.

The Unwritten Rules:

- Dress accordingly. (No duh.)
- Eat only at specific restaurants. (Not a problem, but slightly controlling.)
- Shop only in brand boutiques (Love it.)

- Group functions only. (Meh, let's play this one by ear.)
- No outside friends are allowed. (This is stupid. I'm not pledging a sorority.)
- No sharing of gossip with individuals outside of the group. (Understandable.)

I leaned back in my chair and stared at the list. It was only then, when I saw it written out, that I realized it wasn't normal. We're not a gang or a women's organization, but then again, the rules are not that out there. Well, the rule about no outside friends is stupid, but the other ones seem okay. Maybe it's the "Rules" label that's making me fixated. Maybe I need to look at it like joining a book club. There are rules and whatnot, even if they're not written in stone. But everyone understands that things work a certain way. I focused on another list: the members of our group.

The Roles in a Friend Group:

- Ringleader: Vivian (obviously)
- Dutiful Organizer: Kimmy
- Unofficial Therapist/Mother Figure: Jackie
- Designated Responsible One: Kimmy (again)
- Punching Bag: (Me?)

Was I still being tested and being put through the wringer? Had the group done the same to Meredith? Was that why she kept bringing up the rules? Was that the real reason she wasn't accepted? Did she find the rules ridiculous? Or worse, are there rules I've yet to discover?

Stop, Emily! You have enough issues with your mental health. Why on Earth are you obsessing over this? You're friends with them, not soul mates connected by some unbreakable bond. Save that for Jake.

I sipped my coffee, wondering if the real reason for my overthinking was because I was afraid of becoming attached to Vivian and the others and then not being accepted. Was that it? Was I simply looking for a way to sabotage the relationship just so I could say, "See? I was right."?

You've never acted this way before. Your relationships with your friends were pretty normal, with the expected drama. Why, suddenly, are you tripping over every little issue with these women?

Just then, I received a text message from Kimmy. She wanted to remind me of the time we were meeting for mimosas. I texted Kimmy back, telling her I couldn't wait.

I was looking forward to having mimosas, even though I had just spent most of yesterday with these women. But when I was with them, time flew by. There was never a lull in the conversation. Someone always had something interesting to talk about. So why was it that when I wasn't with them, I started questioning my place within the group? It had to be somehow connected to my past trauma: Noah's death.

I placed my coffee mug in the dishwasher and then took a shower. When I finished, Jake was up and already on his cell phone. He mouthed the name "Kip." From the sound of it, Jake might have to work on Sunday. I felt a little better about having mimosas. I poured him a cup of coffee and placed it in front of him, along with a kiss on his cheek. Then I went and got ready.

"I've got to head into the office today," he said a little later as I sat in front of the mirror, applying my makeup.

"Do you think you'll work late?"

"I don't, so hopefully we can chill later on."

"Is that all you want to do?" I asked with a devilish smile.

"If I tell you what I really want to do, I might not be able to control myself, and I promise you'll have to redo your makeup."

"Save that energy for later."

A little later, Jake and I said our goodbyes, and I made the short walk over to Kimmy's place. She lived in one of the most coveted homes in the community, the closest to me of the three. I chalked it up to the fact that she already had two children when she first arrived in Bangkok. The same went for Jackie. Vivian was the only one with no children I knew of. I still hadn't worked out if she had grown children stashed at college somewhere. She never mentioned this, so it never seemed appropriate to bring it up. Maybe I'd do it today after we'd all had a few mimosas.

Chapter Fifteen

A MONTH HAD FLOWN BY. During that time, I hadn't had a single bad thought about my new friends. I was proud of myself and thought perhaps I'd finally gotten over those immature thoughts. Honestly, a lot of it had to do with the whirlwind life I'd been living. I mean, the benefits of being friends with Vivian, Jackie, and Kimmy by far outweighed any flaws they might have. Admittedly, we all have flaws. Nobody's perfect. I know things about me annoy people, even my husband. But that's life. We accept those things about others if we really want them in our lives.

Being friends with Vivian and the others had given me a glimpse into a world I'd never had the privilege of experiencing. I'd always thought a world like that was made up for TV. But it was true. People flocked to me, tripping over themselves to beg me to attend some function they were holding. Many of them said they would settle for a mention on Instagram. I didn't have an account, but I quickly made one, and within a month I had 250,000 followers. Vivian had just over 700,000, and Jackie and Kimmy were each sitting at half a million. Was I now an influencer? Could posting a picture of myself holding some sort of

The Friend Group

makeup product or attending a restaurant's grand opening really be worth that much to these people? Apparently, the answer was yes.

I was officially, by my estimate, a member of the group. And everyone in Bangkok knew it. I couldn't even believe I'd had doubts about these girls initially. And any whisperings I'd heard about "the rules" I ignored. I chalked it up to those people simply being envious. Plus, everything I learned about navigating any issue or problem here in Bangkok I learned from Vivian, Jackie, or Kimmy. They taught me all the shortcuts and introduced me to the right people who could get stuff done for me. There were absolutely no complaints from me in that department.

If Jake needed something done and couldn't get someone at the office to do it for him, he'd call me. And I handled it, no questions asked. Knowing I could do that was empowering. It made me feel like there was nothing I couldn't do. It was a massive boost to my ego and confidence. I felt like Winston Wolf from *Pulp Fiction*. I was the person you called when you had a problem. And if I did run into a wall, well, I just tapped into Vivian, Jackie, and Kimmy. If I thought *I* held sway, those three were far more resourceful, especially Vivian. I'd never heard anyone tell her no.

One day, we attended the opening of a new boutique shop owned by a local Thai designer. I'd gotten distracted by the store right next door. They sold bougie baby clothes. While I admired the collection through the window, I heard a throat clear. Vivian had come up beside me.

"Lovely clothes, aren't they?" she said.

"Yes, very chic."

She glanced down at my tummy. "Are you pregnant?"

"Oh no, no. I was just admiring the cute outfits."

"Well, I should hope not. You hadn't run it past us."

"Run it past you?" I cocked my head in confusion. "I mean, of course, I would tell you guys. You'd be the first to know."

Just then, someone from the event next door called for us. They wanted us in a picture.

"That's not what I meant," Vivian said, as she started back toward the shop. "Permission, dear." She waved at the person. "We're on the way."

I was left to catch up, with one thought on my mind. Did I just learn of another rule?

Chapter Sixteen

I FINALLY MANAGED to pin down my bestie, Janice, from home. We had each made an effort to schedule a video call into our day that lasted longer than five minutes.

"Oh, my God, I can't believe I'm actually talking to you and you're not in the middle of a mad rush to get out the door to work," I said.

"I know. And I can't believe I'm not waking you out of a deep sleep."

"The stars have aligned," I said.

"Yes, they have. So tell me everything you've been up to. I want to hear it all. My schedule is completely cleared, and I can remain on the phone as long as needed."

I dove into telling Janice about life in Bangkok now that Jake and I had settled into the groove.

"It's amazing. I don't know why I was so worried before."

"It's the unknown; you knew nothing about the place."

"You're right. I kept expecting nothing but rice fields and slow-moving days. It's anything but. Bangkok is a thriving city. The shopping alone is ten times better than in San Francisco."

"Oh, that sounds fun. I need to come out for a visit."

"You should. I know my way around the city now and can be the perfect guide."

"How are things with your new friends? Last we spoke, you were iffy. What was her name? Portia?"

"It's Vivian, and she's amazing, but second to you."

"Of course."

"But seriously, these women have taught me so much about navigating life as an expat. What they've taught me is priceless, plus Vivian is so connected it's unbelievable. The other two, Jackie and Kimmy, are also connected, but not like Vivian. And they've done everything possible to introduce me to the same people."

"Oh, that's so nice of them. Some people wouldn't do that out of insecurity of losing their authority."

"They're not like that. I know enough people that if Jake and I ever have a problem, we can easily handle it. Plus, when you come, be sure to pack an array of party dresses, because I'll get us into all the best ones."

"Love it. I'll be in good hands when I visit."

"I promise not to lose you and have to backtrack my night to find out what happened to you."

Janice let out a huge laugh.

"Is it really a party town?"

"Yeah, it's very much like that movie *The Hangover*, but there's also the other side, the high-society side, which is more like being a socialite in New York, if you know what I mean."

"*The Real Housewives* life?"

"Definitely like that. That's pretty much us daily."

"Oh, I'm so jealous. Ask Jake to get my husband a job at that company. I want to shop and have lunch every day. Becca and I grab a drink occasionally, but I'm usually too tired to do anything after work. It's such a mental drain."

"Who's Becca?"

"Oh, she's this woman I met at a farmers' market. She works in the office building next to mine, so every now and then we'll grab lunch or a drink after work. Don't get jealous. If anyone should be jealous, it's me. I'm the one that's replaceable here."

"Oh, please, you're my oldest and dearest friend. I could never replace you."

"Thank you, dear."

Janice went on to tell me all about the latest with her. She mentioned more names that I wasn't familiar with, as well as doing things that we'd never done together. It was like she was branching out. I sort of expected that our friendship would evolve, but it was a little disheartening to hear about Janice's life moving on. I'm sure she felt the same when she listened to my enthusiastic tales from the Big Mango. Jake had a three-year contract. We'd been here for more than three months, and I already felt some separation between Janice and me. What would our friendship look like three years from now? What if we opted to extend the contract? I decided not to worry about that and just accept the situation. If our bond was strong enough, we'd prevail.

"So, are you and Jake still thinking about trying again?" Janet asked.

"I guess we are. To be honest, Jake's been so busy at work, since the position is new for him, that we haven't had that much sex."

"Are you changing your mind?"

"No, I'm in a good place right now. I've accepted Noah's death and know it has nothing to do with me. I'm ready to try again. It's just that the timing isn't perfect."

"Schedule quickies in the mornings before he goes to work, or tell Jake you both need a break and take off for the weekend. Go explore one of the islands."

"That sounds like a good idea. I'm sure his company can survive a weekend without him."

"Of course they can. Aunt Janice can't wait forever."

"Um..."

"What?"

"It's nothing; forget about it."

"Emily, I've known you too long. Whenever you say 'um,' it's something. Now spit it out."

"Oh, all right. One day I was shopping with Vivian and the others, and I looked at baby outfits in a shop."

"How fun!"

"It was, until Vivian came up to me and asked if I was pregnant. She made it obvious that she was looking at my stomach."

"Okay, and...?"

"I told her I wasn't, but I was admiring the cute outfits. She said 'I hope not' because I didn't run it past them."

"Run it past them? What, like as in ask for approval?"

"Pretty much."

"Are you sure she wasn't implying that she hoped they would be the first to learn the news?"

"That's what I initially thought, and I told her that if I were pregnant, I would tell them as soon as I could."

"And what did she say?"

"We got interrupted just then, but I swear she said telling them wasn't what she meant. She was talking about permission."

"Permission? Why on Earth would you need permission from them to have a baby?"

"You don't know this, so I need to clue you in."

I went ahead and told Janice about the rules in the group.

"I didn't mention it before because I was still confused by what I heard. I couldn't tell if it was dumb gossip, normal unwritten rules we all have, or something more serious."

"I'm sure it's just the unwritten rule thing."

"That's what Jake said."

"Did you ask them?"

"I eventually did mention something to Vivian. This lady I met from Australia was constantly making a big deal out of the rules, so I told Vivian about it. She told me not to believe anything that woman said because she was a huge gossip. She even said that woman tried to become friends with Vivian and the others, but it didn't work out."

"She sounds bitter."

"You and Jake are saying the same thing."

"Great minds think alike. But these 'rules' sound more like something Miss Manners would say, like common sense. Dressing appropriately or lunching in the right spots makes sense, considering their position in the community. These women seem like they're well respected."

"They are—like, insanely. Even Vivian mentioned to me that I always need to be aware of my surroundings and what I say to people."

"Are you okay with it?"

"I am, because the benefits are out of this world."

"Honestly, these rules seem like rules every friendship has."

"But what about the pregnancy rule?"

"I'm sure she misspoke. Or maybe she was joking. I'd forget about it and just do you. It seems like they've already accepted you as one of the gang. Did you mention the pregnancy thing to Jake?"

"No, you're the first I've told."

"Well, I wouldn't worry yourself over it. Go make a baby if you want to. You have Aunt Janice's permission."

Chapter Seventeen

It was a Thursday night, and I was on my way to meet the group at a function at the top of the Mahanakhon skyscraper. It had seventy-seven floors, and the rooftop boasted three 360-degree views of Bangkok. But what made it stand out against the skyline was the architecture, which featured a pixelated cut on the side of the building. I'd always referred to it as the Lego building and had added it to my list of places to visit. So, when this event popped up, I was excited to attend.

Lately, Kimmy and I had been sharing a car to events since our places were a stone's throw away, but that day she had a hair appointment before the event. She said she'd meet me there. The trek up to the top floor had me pass through three checkpoints. I was confident there wouldn't be a problem, because I'd been to enough of these events that my face and name had grown familiar to the security people. I'm sure it helped that I always tipped as I passed through.

I was the first of our group to arrive. I headed over to the bar and got myself a glass of champagne. The owner of ThaiBev, the largest beverage company in Thailand, hosted the event. He wanted to celebrate the founding of his new football club in the English Premier League.

I wasn't a big fan of football (or soccer, as we call it in the States), but the players who were at the event were not bad on the eyes. Jackie was the first of the three to arrive. Kimmy appeared shortly after.

We stood to one side, sipping champagne as we talked about our days. That's when Vivian appeared. She had a troubled look on her face as she approached us.

"Hey, Vivian," Jackie said. "Is something bothering you?"

"There is." She came to a stop, drew a breath, and calmed herself. "It appears that what we talk about among ourselves has found its way to prying ears. Someone has loose lips."

Right then, everyone in the group looked at me.

"We are a tight group," Vivian said. "We talk freely and openly, and we do so because we know what we say stays among us. But it only works if we all follow the rule."

No one said a word, but I knew everyone thought the leak came from me.

"Um, I might have mentioned to Meredith about a get-together we were having at Kimmy's," I said. "But that was a while back. I didn't think it was that big of a deal."

"As I've said before, this expat community can be vicious, and fake news spreads fast. I can't tell you how many people have been forced to leave this town because of it."

"What do you mean by 'leave'?" I asked.

"They picked up and left Thailand," Kimmy said.

"It's true," Jackie said. "I've seen it happen."

"Just from people gossiping?" I said.

"It's not just people in the expat community. It's the Thai community, as well. If the Thais ostracize you, forget about it. Life becomes challenging here. Sure, you can shield yourself by remaining in our community, but eventually, it becomes too much."

"So they, like, left the country?"

"It just happened a few months ago," Vivian said. "One minute, they were here. The next minute, they were gone, never to be heard from again."

"Where did they go?" I asked.

"Good question." Vivian stared me down. "People disappear all the time."

"But all the Thai people I've met seemed so happy and nice."

"If there's one thing I know to be true," Kimmy said, "a smiling Thai doesn't mean they're happy or nice."

Vivian and Jackie nodded.

"I hope this is clear for you, Emily," Vivian said. "We'd hate to lose you."

Lose me? Is she for real?

"The four of us are the only ones looking out for us. Saying nothing is one more layer of protection. Is that clear to everyone?"

But what about the pregnancy rule? What does that have to do with the gossip mill?

I mimicked zipping my mouth shut while Jackie and Kimmy nodded.

"I hope this is the last time we speak of this," said Vivian, looking at Kimmy's glass of champagne. "May I?"

"Yes, of course."

Vivian took the glass and finished it in one gulp. "Well, now that we got that out of the way, let's do what we do best: wow the people here."

And just like that, smiles appeared as they spread out to work the crowd. I stood there, confused. Sure, what Vivian said made sense when she put it that way, but still, it wasn't like I'd divulged a secret one of us had told the group. I wasn't that stupid.

I also didn't like Vivian's tone. It was very authoritative, like we were her minions. I shrugged it off. Vivian could be over the top at times, but she was the one who had worked hard to establish our group's status. Maybe that's where this was all coming from.

"Hey Emily, fancy seeing you here."

I turned to find Meredith smiling at me.

"I'm just kidding you. I know you come to all these events. Are you here alone?" she asked, as she looked around.

"No, I'm here with Vivian, Jackie, and Kimmy. They just left to mingle."

"Of course, why would you come alone?"

"Are you here with someone?" I asked.

"Yes, another employee at the Australian embassy."

"Meredith, I have a question for you. How is it you're able to work?"

"Technically, you can't just go out and get a job. You need to obtain a work permit, which I'm sure you could easily wangle if you wanted. Why, are you having financial problems? Do you want me to spread the word that you desperately need a job?"

"No, Meredith. I only asked out of curiosity."

I understood right then and there what Vivian was talking about. Meredith was practically foaming at the mouth with that tidbit.

She'll probably spread that rumor anyway.

Just then, Kimmy waved me over to her.

"Don't be a stranger," said Meredith. "We should grab coffee sometime."

"Yeah, sure. DM me on Instagram."

"Oh, okay. Yeah, I can do that."

I hurried over to Kimmy and mouthed "thank you" when I was close enough.

"Was Meredith pumping you for information?"

If it were any other situation, I would have said no, because asking questions is normal and part of the conversation. Still, given the scolding from Vivian, I could see how it looked.

"I made the mistake of asking her how she could work, and that suddenly turned into her thinking Jake and I are in financial trouble and that I now desperately need a job."

Kimmy rolled her eyes. "That is so Meredith. This is exactly what Vivian was talking about earlier. She knows best."

"She does, doesn't she?"

I quickly thought that now might be a good time to bring up the pregnancy rule, seeing that we were alone and discussing the rules.

"Any other rules I should know about? I don't want to do something stupid."

"Um, it's not like we have bylaws written down someplace. It's mostly just common sense. And because you're still new to the Bangkok scene, it makes sense that you still need to learn things. That's why it feels like we have rules."

"Yeah, that makes sense."

But none of those rules come even close to needing permission to get pregnant.

"How do you like your nanny?" I asked.

"Oh, she's great. I don't know what I would do without her. She's a lifesaver."

"Is she Thai?"

"Yes, but her English is excellent. I never have any problems communicating with her, nor do the kids. In fact, because they're young, they can pick up Thai easily."

"Oh, is that something you're trying to do?"

"Absolutely. I want them to experience as much as possible.

And being bilingual is cool. I wish I could speak more than one language. You know, some kids at their school are fluent in four languages. Can you imagine that?"

"That's amazing."

"Wait!" Kimmy grabbed my arm. "You're not pregnant, are you?"

"No, no. I was just making conversation."

"Are you and Jake planning to have kids?"

None of the girls knew about Noah or the therapy I needed to help me cope. I didn't think it was their business, at least not at the moment. Maybe at some point in time, I might have shared that with them.

"We've talked about it, but nothing serious. Jake is very career-focused right now."

"Aren't all our husbands? But that's part of the deal. Big salaries require long hours."

"Exactly. That's why I was asking about your nanny. It's not common back in the States, but everyone here has one."

"I know what you mean. I thought the same thing when I first got here. I resisted the thought of hiring someone to look after my children. My initial instinct was that I didn't need help. They're my children. I can take care of them just fine. But the more I learned about what a nanny could do for me, the more open to the idea I became. Don't get me wrong, I was still against it, but eventually, I fell into line."

"What was the deciding factor that made you get a nanny?"

"Vivian."

Chapter Eighteen

A FEW DAYS had passed since the event at the Mahanakhon tower. I was probably overreacting, but I couldn't shake the feeling that the discussion about keeping our conversations in the group private was about me and not just a reminder of the rules. When I first met Meredith, she mentioned I'd taken the revolving seat. I didn't think much of it until now.

Was my spot in the group on shaky ground?

Meredith had tried to join the group. Vivian said she didn't vibe with the others. Maybe it was true, maybe not. Meredith, as a gossiper, was doomed from the start. Vivian nearly chewed my head off for speaking out of line. I guessed Meredith was kicked out for having loose lips and not because she didn't vibe. I wondered how many other women auditioned for the role of the fourth chair.

What are you doing, Emily? Why are you even giving these thoughts any energy? Who cares how many people had your seat before you? Meredith mentioned the revolving chair because she's petty and jealous that she didn't win over the group.

My therapist always told me if I ever feel like I'm getting stuck in my own thoughts, I should get out of the house for a brisk walk. "You'd be amazed what fresh air and a warming sun can do for your mindset," she'd told me.

She'd come to know me in ways most people didn't. I trusted her advice. One day, I asked her if she thought I was crazy. She said I simply had an overactive imagination that led to overthinking, which led to me creating alternative realities. It sounds a lot worse than it really is. She said everyone was guilty of it but that I did it more than most. Her job was to help me recognize when I did it and that, in time, I would be able to control myself.

Noah's passing didn't help matters. She said, "We often overanalyze a situation or problem in hopes of helping ourselves work through an issue, especially if we have no one we can talk to." That summed up my situation.

She mentioned that's the number one reason why we start conversations with ourselves. I was totally guilty of that. The problem with that, she said, was, "People will pose a question and then answer it. By doing so, we give ourselves the answer we want." This was what fueled my grief hallucinations. I hadn't accepted Noah's death, so my brain compensated for it by giving me the answer I wanted. Which was Noah.

That was my issue with all these rules. My overactive imagination was hard at work and gave me the answer I wanted: I wasn't good enough to be a part of this fantastic friend group and was going to be cut. Self-sabotage at its finest.

Since I had no plans that day and Jake was at work, I went out for a walk. I had no set place in mind and decided to roam. After a solid thirty minutes in a direction I had never gone before, I stumbled across a local day market. It was the perfect distraction for me.

In addition to vendors selling fresh veggies and fruit, there were also a bunch selling sweets, ice cream, smoothies, juices, and crafts. I bought a cup of coconut ice cream and sat on a bench, happy to people-watch while I ate. I was scooping the last bite when I heard a voice.

"Excuse me. Is it okay if I sit here?"

I looked up and found a smiling woman with an armful of bags.

"Yes, of course." I scooted over.

She took a seat and placed her bags down before closing her eyes and turning her face up to the sky. Her smooth brown skin glowed in the sun, and her long black hair was held back in a ponytail by a plastic clip. She looked to be in her mid-thirties. But I learned that Thai people always looked younger than their actual age.

"It's such a nice day today," she said, her eyes still closed. "Perfect for the market."

"It is. This is my first time coming here."

She opened her eyes. "I've been coming here for the past year." She motioned to all of the fruits and veggies she had bought. "I usually come once a week to stock up. Do you live in the area?"

"About a thirty-minute walk in that direction," I pointed. "And you?"

"Not far, about a ten-minute walk."

"It's very convenient for you."

"Very much. If you don't mind me asking, where are you from? You're American, right?"

"Yes, I'm from San Francisco. My husband and I moved here about three months ago."

"How are you liking it so far?"

"I love it. I won't lie; there was a bit of a learning curve in the beginning. I've never lived outside of the United States, but now I know my way around."

"That's good to hear." She smiled as she extended her hand. "My name is Sasithorn, but you can call me Sasi, like sassy."

"I'm Emily. It's nice to meet you. I hope this doesn't come across as offensive, but you speak English with no accent."

"When I was younger, I studied at the international schools in Bangkok, and then I moved to New York to attend Columbia University, where I eventually got my medical degree. I did my residency in Chicago."

"Wow. That explains it all."

"Yes. About ten years ago, I returned to Thailand and started my own practice."

"What kind of medicine do you practice?"

"I'm an OB-GYN."

"Oh, how cool."

"And yourself?"

"I'm afraid I'm not nearly as accomplished as you. Right now, I'm a housewife. My husband was the one with the job offer here. So that's it in a nutshell."

Sasi and I talked a bit longer before she suggested having lunch together. I enjoyed our conversation, so I agreed.

"It's a lovely Thai restaurant I like to visit after shopping at the market," she said as she led the way. "It's about a five-minute walk from here. And they have fresh coconut water. My favorite."

"Me too!"

Our lunch extended into coffee at another location, because we were having a great time. Sasi was an exciting person. On the one hand, I could relate to her as an American because of her time there. On the other, hearing her talk about her upbringing in Thailand was equally enjoyable. Sasi was the first Thai person I'd met with whom I felt a real, honest discussion was taking place. I hated to admit it, but most of my conversations with Thai people so far had been at the events. Those conversations were almost always transactional: something for something.

It turned out Sasi was forty-one, though she didn't look it. She came from a family of scholars. They weren't wealthy, but her father had always put a lot of emphasis on education, telling her it was the next best thing to having money.

"We lived a comfortable and normal life," she said. "But it was nothing like the hi-so Thais. My parents sacrificed a lot to make sure we had the best education possible."

"Where are your parents now?"

"They both passed."

"I'm sorry to hear that."

"Thank you. My younger sister is married and living in Japan. My younger brother is married and living in the UK. I'm the only one here in Thailand and the single one in the family." She laughed.

"I can't believe it. You're so beautiful. I would have thought you'd have an army of men chasing you around."

I wasn't exaggerating when I said that. I thought Sasi was stunning and half expected her to tell me she picked up English while modeling worldwide.

"The truth is I'm unable to have children," she said. "For Thai men, that's a relationship killer."

"Oh, I'm sorry. I didn't mean to pry."

"It's quite all right. I occasionally go out on dates, mostly with foreigners. But honestly, my work makes me happy and takes up much of my time. I rejected three marriage proposals while I was younger and living in the U.S."

"Three? You're a heartbreaker," I said, laughing.

"I'm not an easy catch, that's for sure, but back to becoming an OB-GYN, I figured if I couldn't have children, I could at least help other women have healthy and successful pregnancies."

I knew that if Vivian, Jackie, or Kimmy saw me right now, it would not go over well. But I didn't care. I was thoroughly enjoying my time with Sasi. That rule about no outside friendships was stupid. I could be friends with anyone I want.

By the time we said goodbye to each other, we had exchanged contact information and agreed to meet the next day. I walked away happy, and not once during that time had I thought about the rules.

Chapter Nineteen

I HAD the best week ever. During the day, I hung out with Sasi, and at night, I attended these fabulous events with the girls. And now it was Friday, and Jake had the next four days off, so we were flying to one of the islands for some relaxation and quality time together.

"I'm so excited!" I said, clutching Jake's arm as we touched down on Koh Samui.

Not only were we embarking on what I was sure would be a fabulous vacation, but Jake's boss, Kip, had called a contact at the Four Seasons and gotten us into a beach villa with a private pool. And the best part was that Jake's company was taking care of the villa's cost.

"I can't believe your boss did this for us," I said as we climbed into the car that had been sent from the hotel to pick us up. "They must be really happy with you."

"That, and I'm busting my butt for them."

"Yes, you are, and I want you to know I appreciate every single second of your butt-busting efforts."

Just then, I got a text message from Vivian wishing us an amazing time and asking us to send photos to the group chat.

"That was nice of her," Jake said. "How are things with you and the gang?"

"We're fine."

"Yeah, and the rules?"

"Meh, I was simply overthinking stuff. I've moved on."

"That's good to hear. I'm glad all is well, and you're keeping busy. I know you're alone a lot."

"Actually, I'm not."

"I mean, I know I work a lot."

"It's fine, honey. You're still proving your worth, which seems to be paying off. You'll hear no complaints from me."

Our villa was much more impressive in person. The pictures on the website were incredible but paled in comparison to the real thing. The private pool was perfect, and, we also had a private beach.

"This has got to be the nicest place we have ever stayed at," I said.

"I second that. I need to send Kip a thank you." Jake pulled out his phone and began tapping out a message. "Come over here. Let's take a picture for him."

Jake snapped a picture of our smiling faces with the beach as our backdrop and then sent it off.

"So what should we do first?" I asked.

"I know this will sound totally cheesy, but I say we christen the bed."

Jake didn't even wait for me to answer before he scooped me up in his arms.

"Wait, all the windows and the balcony doors are open," I said. "People will be able to see us."

"What people?" he asked as he started undressing me. "That beach is completely deserted."

"But..."

"We're on vacation. We're supposed to be wild and crazy."

After our fun quickie, I watched Jake play on the beach from the balcony. He was doing handstands and yelling out for me to make a video. I'd bet him earlier that he couldn't.

"Are you filming me?" he shouted.

I went down the stairs, past our pool, and onto the beach. He looked cute with his upside-down grin, like a proud little boy who had just won a significant bet, the stakes being more sex. Of course, if I had won, we'd go shopping. We'd probably still go.

Jake had always been easy to please. Simple things made him happy. Placing a hotdog in his hand when he didn't ask for one turned me into a saint. I would have done it for him regardless. I loved taking care of him, watching over him, doting whenever I could. He might not know it, but I was always thinking about him, making sure he had everything he needed. It was an easy job. Jake was self-sufficient, so there wasn't much left for me to do. If he needed something, he often went out and got it. Occasionally, he'd ask me to order something online, but only sometimes. He picked up after himself and did the dishes, if any were in the sink. He loaded the washing machine if there were clothes in the hamper and folded them if they were sitting in the dryer. I'd never had to get on him to help around the house. That's why I made him snacks when he wasn't expecting it. I loved watching that smile grow on his face when I placed food in front of him. He even did a little dance where he shimmied his shoulders before taking his first bite. It was cute.

I had always told Janice that I hit the jackpot when I married Jake. Because I almost didn't. Not because I wasn't sure if I wanted to spend the rest of my life with him. I did. What scared me, what had me wanting to run away, was myself. You see, I'm not always in control of my actions.

Chapter Twenty

Client: Emily Platt
Therapist: Dr. Tammy Young
Therapy Session #: 22

Data:
Emily arrived early to our session. She was visibly happy and eager to get started. She talked about a new job doing admin work. She likes the people at the company and said her supervisor was friendly. Jake had suggested that she get a job so she wasn't cooped up in the house all day. She admits that keeping busy and being around others has helped her deal with the loss of Noah. She's accepted that it was an unfortunate accident and not something she or Jake were responsible for. She realizes she blamed Jake at first, but that was only because she thought someone had to be blamed, and she couldn't live with herself if she felt she was responsible. Emily knows she and Jake did everything they could to ensure a healthy pregnancy. She says she will never forget Noah, and he will live in her heart, but she knows she needs to live for herself. When I asked if they'd

discussed the idea of trying again, she said they had. She said they're both ready to bring a child into their lives. She tells me she's ready to move on from our therapy sessions.

Assessment:
Emily has made a great deal of improvement since our first meeting. She has come to accept what has happened. More importantly, she no longer blames Jake or herself for what happened. But I don't believe her. I think the Emily that shows up for our sessions is putting on a performance. She appears too perfect and too eager to please me. My receptionist has reported that while sitting in the waiting room, Emily is often agitated. Her demeanor changes when she enters my office. I believe there is more at play here besides her grief. I've noted signs of schizophrenia and want to continue to monitor this. Grief may not be the underlying reason for her behavior.

Plan:
Recommend that Emily continue the sessions. I want to assess what happens once she and Jake start trying and if Emily becomes pregnant. There is a possibility for a relapse at that point.

Chapter Twenty-One

"Hi, Emily," Sasi said as she leaned in and hugged me. "I'm sorry I'm late for lunch. I had to attend to a patient unexpectedly."

"Is everything all right with her?"

"She's fine. It's her first pregnancy, and she's nervous."

My friendship with Sasi had blossomed since our meeting at the market. She was so down to earth and chill that I didn't feel like I needed to think about how I looked around her, what I said, or even how I talked with a mouthful of food. With Vivian and the others, it was different because of who they were and how our friend group was perceived in Bangkok. I loved being a part of both and wouldn't want to trade one for the other.

But I had put myself in a pickle. Vivian and the others didn't know about Sasi. I was sure it would raise eyebrows if they found out. No outside friends. That was a rule. And it wasn't one I really agreed with.

However, I didn't like drama, so I'd hidden my friendship with Sasi. I was careful of where we met, where we shopped and ate. Luckily, Sasi wasn't a part of the Bangkok hi-so scene and had no aspirations to integrate herself into it. But she was aware that I was friends with Vivian. It slipped one day while we were having coffee. Rather than cover it up, I dug to see what she knew.

"Do you know Vivian?" I had asked.

"I know of her...through a colleague who treated her at the hospital," she'd said.

All expats in Thailand patronize the Royal International Hospital, a private hospital that cares for patients all across Southeast Asia and the Middle East. Those who want the best care and can afford it go there. Thankfully, Jake's company paid for our medical coverage, so that was where we went for treatment.

I wasn't surprised that Sasi knew of Vivian. She was a prominent figure in the expat community.

While Sasi looked over the menu, I couldn't help but think our friendship was both a blessing and a curse. In any normal situation, it wouldn't even be an issue who I kept company with. But life in Bangkok was anything but ordinary.

"Do you know what you're having?" I asked.

"They have my favorite here: yum sum o. Have you tried it?"

"I don't think I have."

"It's a refreshing salad made with pomelo with a little bit of chili kick to it."

"That sounds delicious."

"It does. Let's split one."

"Sounds great."

"Do you want to have a wine spritzer?"

"Um..."

"A white wine spritzer would pair nicely with the salad."

"I'm sure it would, but I'll take a rain check."

Sasi looked up from the menu. "What's wrong?"

"Nothing's wrong. I just, I don't know, it's a bit early for alcohol."

Sasi glanced at her watch. "Uh, we drank together much earlier than this... Wait." Sasi crinkled her brow as she stared at me. She suddenly slapped her hand across her mouth and leaned across the table. "Are you pregnant?"

"What?"

"You're pregnant, aren't you?"

"Whatever gave you that idea? Just because I don't want to drink doesn't mean I'm pregnant."

Sasi raised a brow. "I've been an OB-GYN long enough to know. It's a secret power of mine." She eyed me for a bit. "And you have that pregnant glow."

"Pregnant glow?"

"Yes, so stop trying to play it off like I'm some dummy."

I glanced around quickly as a smile formed on my face. "You got me. I'm pregnant."

Sasi squealed. "Oh my God, I'm so happy for you and Jake. How far along are you?"

"A little more than a month and a half. I missed my period and started thinking I might be. I must have taken about a dozen home pregnancy tests. All of them were positive."

"Have you gone to the hospital for a checkup yet?"

"I haven't. In fact, I haven't even told Jake."

"Why not?"

"I wanted to be sure because I know he'll be over the moon. That and I'm still trying to process it myself."

"You'll make a great mother. I know it."

"I really hope so."

"I'm sensing in your voice there's more than just the need to process."

"There is something else that I haven't mentioned to you or anyone here in Thailand."

I told Sasi about my first pregnancy and how difficult it had been to have a healthy baby boy, only to lose him months later to SIDS.

"Oh, Emily. I am so sorry to hear about that. The pain you must have experienced... I'm sorry."

"Thank you. That's the real reason why I'm hesitant. I just don't want a repeat. With that first pregnancy, there was a real concern that I might miscarry. I know I'm at higher risk the second time, and if I must remain in bed, I will, but..."

"Emily, you need to stop having these negative thoughts. Positivity is all I want from you from this point forward. From what I can tell, you lead a healthy lifestyle, but more importantly, you have a stress-free life. These negative thoughts you're having will bring stress into your life and affect your mood, which affects your appetite and willingness to exercise, but more importantly, it can cause you to dip into depression. Your mental health is important and key to a successful pregnancy. And by the way, I don't believe your previous experience automatically increases your odds for a difficult pregnancy."

"But the last time, I was feeling healthy, and then I developed a problem with the placenta and—"

"Emily, what did I just say? You must remain positive. Don't start comparing this pregnancy to the last one. It'll only drive you nuts. Instead, I want you to come to me with any questions or concerns. Okay?"

"Thank you, Sasi. It means a lot to hear that."

"Of course. You're my friend. I'll do whatever you need to ensure you end up with a healthy baby."

Right then, I was delighted to have Sasi in my life. There was no way I would get rid of her because of some stupid rule Vivian came up with. Sasi seemed genuinely happy for me, beaming at me from across the table. I wasn't sure I would have the same reaction from the group.

The Friend Group

Later that night, I shared the good news with Jake. After a few minutes of jumping up and down and fist-pumping, Jake calmed down enough to hug and kiss me.

"I knew I impregnated you while we were in Koh Samui."

"Impregnated?" I laughed. "What makes you so sure it was during that weekend?"

"I felt strong that weekend." He winked at me.

I told Jake about my conversation with Sasi earlier in the day and how she sniffed it out.

"Well, she's an OB-GYN. She would know. But I agree with everything she told you." Jake took me into his arms. "You shouldn't compare pregnancies."

"I know, but it's just that...you know what I mean."

"I do, but I think listening to what Sasi has to say is the right way. We need to remain positive and have happy thoughts. You had a tough time after we lost Noah, but you're better now. Let's not lose all that progress." Jake kissed me on the forehead.

I really appreciated his support, but I just knew how I could be. I knew what I was. I knew I had fooled my therapist, my best friend, Janice, and even my husband. I hadn't gotten better. In fact, I might just have gotten a bit worse.

Chapter Twenty-Two

Since the day that both Jake and Sasi became aware of my pregnancy, I proceeded forward as if nothing were different with me. Whenever I was around Vivian and the girls, I acted the same way as always. I had gotten clever with alcohol since it was readily available at the functions we attended. Rather than outright refuse a drink, which would undoubtedly tip them off, I'd either nurse one, pretending to take sips, or I'd order my own drink when they weren't around and make it non-alcoholic. My gin and tonics were gin-free. And on one occasion, I kept emptying my glass into a potted plant. I did decline some functions, stating I was tired or already had plans with Jake. So far, none of my actions had raised a red flag.

I wasn't sure how I would break the news to them. I kept thinking about those stupid rules, especially the one where I was supposed to ask permission to be pregnant. Give me a break. But I swore that was precisely what Vivian implied that day when she said to run it past them. The subject hadn't come up since, but sooner or later, I would start showing and, well, there's no hiding a baby bump.

One Sunday morning, I received a call from Vivian.

"Emily dear, where are you? We're all here at Jackie's, drinking mimosas. Why haven't you joined us?"

"I must have missed that message," I said.

"Well, now you know. Come over."

In the background, I could hear Jackie and Kimmy pleading with me to come.

"You see, we all miss you."

I racked my brain for an acceptable excuse that they would all buy, but all I could come up with was, "I uh, um, uh."

"We'll see you soon," Vivian said before disconnecting the call.

Crap!

I dressed and made my way over while scheming how I would get out of drinking. I decided to grab a cup of coffee from Starbucks and use that as my defense.

When I arrived at Jackie's place, I was greeted with hugs and kisses. Everyone seemed to be in an exceptional mood that day.

"Put that coffee down," Jackie said. "I'll fix you a mimosa."

"Not now. I really need the caffeine, or I'm afraid I'll fall asleep on you guys."

"What's wrong?" Kimmy asked. "Are you having trouble sleeping?"

"A little; it's nothing to worry about. I think it's a phase."

"Well, maybe you need a drink," Vivian said. "A mimosa without the orange juice."

"I'm fine with my coffee. So, everyone is in a bubbly mood today," I said, desperately trying to change the subject.

"Emily?" Vivian eyed me momentarily. "You're not pregnant, are you?"

Kimmy slapped a hand across her mouth. "Oh, my God! Are you pregnant?"

"You're not drinking. You're pregnant!" Jackie shouted as she straightened up.

"Please. I had a drink with you all just a few nights ago at that architecture party. Don't you remember?"

"Oh, that's right." Jackie's posture deflated.

"Are you sure?" Vivian asked, continuing to fan the flame as she looked at my belly.

Needle me all you want, Vivian. I'll keep telling one lie after another.

"I'm sure. Lately, I've had killer headaches. Jake thinks I'm not drinking enough water."

"I agree with him," Jackie said. "Two large bottles of water a day keep me hydrated. You should do the same. But don't try to drink that water all at once. Spread it out through the day."

"Oh, and if your pee is clear, then you're drinking enough," Kimmy said.

I glanced over at Vivian, and she was eyeing me suspiciously. I might have thrown Jackie and Kimmy off the trail, but I wasn't sure I'd convinced Vivian.

For the rest of the morning, I felt guilty for keeping my pregnancy from them. I wanted to share this happy moment, but I couldn't stop thinking about the rule. Thankfully I had Sasi in my life. She provided emotional support that I couldn't quite get from Vivian, Jackie, or Kimmy. At least not when the four of us were together. But having Sasi also complicated matters. I didn't want to have to hide her.

I managed to get through the rest of the morning without any more questioning and ended up enjoying myself. When I came home, Jake asked how it went. He knew I wasn't supposed to be drinking.

"It was fun, and don't worry, I didn't drink a mimosa."

"I wasn't worried. Did you tell them?"

"No."

"Is it because of that comment Vivian made?"

"Of course it is. I'm not sure how to handle it."

"Look, sweetie. If these women are your friends, they'll be happy for you."

"But what Vivian said—"

"Forget about what Vivian said. I'm sure it's not how it sounded."

"You weren't there, Jake. And you didn't see that look on her face."

"I wasn't, but there's no turning back now. Soon you'll start showing. Telling them is inevitable."

"I know, I'm just waiting for the right moment, like when it's obvious. Do you think that's bad?"

"No, lots of couples wait until after four months to start telling people. Plus, it's our decision, not theirs. I'm sure they'll be happy when you do tell them."

"I think I'll wait until I have a noticeable bump."

"Fine. I'm on board with whatever you want to do."

I headed into our bedroom to lie down for a bit. There was one thing I had to do, and that was to find a new OB-GYN. The one I saw at the expat hospital was fine, but there was too much risk in continuing to see her. Sooner or later, word would get out about my visits and make its way back to the group. I couldn't think of anyone better to replace my current doctor than my friend Sasi.

Chapter Twenty-Three

For some reason, I had been expecting Sasi's practice to be housed in a quaint little office on the first floor of an old building. I couldn't have been more wrong. She had her own two-story, standalone office that was about the size of a large ranch home. The front of the office had large glass windows with tinted panes. The signage was discreet, and it didn't have photos of smiling women and babies plastered on the outside like many of the maternal health clinics here did.

The woman at reception smiled at me as I walked in. "Swadeeka."

"Swadeeka," I said. "I'm here to see Dr. Chaidee. I'm Emily Platt."

The waiting room was small, with just a few chairs and couches. The walls were covered with photos of what I assumed were mothers and their newborns, most likely all the babies Sasi had helped deliver. After a short wait, an aide escorted me back to an examination room and told me to change out of my clothes and into a gown. A few minutes later, Sasi entered the room. I was surprised to see her looking so professional, as I'd never seen her dressed in a white lab coat.

"Hi, Emily." She gave me a quick hug. "I'm so excited to be overseeing your pregnancy. I promise you'll be in good hands."

"I have all the confidence in the world in you."

"Besides that, I'm an awesome OB-GYN."

Sasi washed her hands, snapped on a pair of gloves, and proceeded to give me a complete checkup.

"Do you want to share why you came here?" she asked.

"Well, you're my friend, and I trust you."

"Of course."

"And I want to be with someone I know, someone who makes me comfortable. You did that the day I confided in you about my previous pregnancy."

"But..." Sasi peered up at me.

"But what?"

"Are you sure this isn't about your other friends?"

"Um..."

"It's fine, Emily. I am not all that concerned about why you've come to me. I'm just happy that you did and that we're both on the same page: delivering a healthy baby."

"We are. You said my mental health will play a large role in avoiding a difficult pregnancy."

"That's correct."

"So, I chose to avoid the stress of sneaking in and out of the Royal International Hospital. I want people to find out on my terms, not through the grapevine. This is my decision. Period. Switching doctors isn't that big of a deal."

"It's not."

"And most couples wait until after the first trimester anyway to say something to people."

"I sense a big part of this move was to prevent your other friends from finding out."

I let out a breath. "It is."

"You've decided not to say anything to them?"

"Only for the time being."

"Your instincts were right about that hospital," Sasi said as she slipped off her gloves and tossed them into a trash bin. "A lot of whispering goes on there. If privacy is what you want, you'll get it here. You can hide a baby bump with smart choices in your wardrobe, but eventually, you'll waddle around like all pregnant women."

"I know. I'm just not sure when and how to tell them."

"You still have time. It won't seem out of the ordinary to keep it a secret for now." Sasi started writing notes in my chart.

I loved that she was so understanding. She didn't seem to think it was a big deal to keep quiet about my pregnancy. It's common for couples to wait. It is even more common to wait longer if they had a problematic previous pregnancy. Of course, Vivian and the others knew nothing about that. Sasi knew, but she didn't know about the other underlying reason: the rule.

"Well, if you want my take on it, I don't see why being pregnant is such a big deal. What are they going to do? Tell you to stop being pregnant?"

"Um, that isn't very far off."

Sasi stopped writing and looked up at me. "What are you talking about?"

"Remember how I told you that group had these unwritten rules we're supposed to follow?"

"Yes."

"There's a rule, no unapproved pregnancies."

"That's ridiculous."

"I agree, but it's true."

"Wait, they told you permission is needed to have a baby? Permission by whom?"

"Them. I know it sounds crazy, but Vivian asked if I was pregnant one day because I was admiring baby outfits in the store. I wasn't sure if it was a joke, but I told her no because I wasn't then."

"And what did she say?"

I thought back to the moment because I wanted to get her response right.

"Her exact words were, 'I should hope not. You hadn't run it past us.'"

"Run it past them?" Sasi cocked her head in confusion. "What does that mean?"

"That was my exact reaction. I thought either I had heard wrong or she meant something else. So, of course, I asked her to clarify. But just then, someone from the event we were at interrupted us. They needed us for a picture. Vivian had already turned her attention to that person. As she walked away, she said, 'That's not what I meant. Permission, dear.'"

Sasi drew a sharp breath. "You're kidding!"

"I'm not. I swear she said 'permission.'"

"Did you say something back?"

"No, because a few seconds later, we were being corralled into a photo session, and then there were all these people around us, so it wasn't an ideal time to pick up the conversation again."

"It all makes sense, the move over here. Because the OB-GYNs at the Royal International Hospital are excellent."

"I know, but I didn't want Vivian and the others to find out from some random person. I guess I was buying myself time."

"Understandable. Did you try bringing it up again later with her?"

"No, because it never seemed like a good time, and then it seemed like old news. I wasn't pregnant, and Jake and I weren't seriously trying. It just happened. Now I'm pregnant, and I don't know how to tell them. What do you think I should do?"

"First off, it's no one's business but yours. Secondly, if they really are your friends, they'll be happy for you."

"That's exactly what Jake said."

"Great minds think alike," Sasi said with a smile. "Look, you still have time without it looking like you held out on them."

"I know."

"But as your OB-GYN, I want to voice a concern. Don't overthink this. It's not that big of a deal. I don't want you stressing out. It can raise your blood pressure. Do you understand?"

"I understand. Thank you."

"Enough of that drama; let's talk about something more important and fun. Today I'll be giving you an ultrasound. If I can determine it, and I might not be able to, do you want to know the sex of your baby?"

"Of course. I want to start planning the room."

"Perfect."

Chapter Twenty-Four

Client: Emily Platt
Therapist: Dr. Tammy Young
Therapy Session #: 24

Data:
Emily arrived on time with a smile. I asked her why she was in such a good mood, and she told me she was excited about her first scheduled play date for Noah. She tells me that even though he's too young to enjoy it, she thinks it'll be a good idea for Noah and her to do things outside the house. When I asked about her admin job, she looked at me as if I had her confused with someone else. I gently reminded her about the job and how much she enjoyed it. Just as she started to protest about not working, she lost her train of thought. I told her she was talking about her job, which she continued to talk about for the next fifteen minutes. She didn't remember mentioning Noah or his play date when I mentioned it. She immediately became distraught, and I explained to her that she isn't regressing and

that there is no one right way to move through the cycles of grief, nor is it mandatory that she move through all five.

Assessment:
Emily has reverted backward in her grieving cycle. There is some concern, but grief isn't always linear, and this behavior can be common with extreme grief, such as Emily's. This could just be a one-time occurrence, or it may be a signal that she's not coping as well as I had thought. However, my concern lies with her state of mind. Emily shows signs of schizophrenia. I want Emily to see another doctor who would be better equipped to diagnose Emily's schizophrenia and provide treatment if deemed necessary.

Plan:
Recommend Emily continue the sessions with me and see another therapist. Watch for signs or indicators that she's acting on her grief hallucinations, e.g., showing up at a park or a friend's house believing she's there for a play date or buying items for Noah. Continue to monitor her self-doubt about getting better. If she continues down this path, ask Emily that we share this with her husband or have a separate session with him.

Chapter Twenty-Five

Since I had time on my hands and full mobility, I decided to be proactive. I headed to the U.S. embassy to learn what I needed to do to obtain U.S. citizenship for my child. Giving birth in Thailand wasn't that big of a deal, according to Sasi. She mentioned having a baby here was the same as in the States. All I would need to do was file the proper paperwork for my child afterward.

I arrived at the embassy in the morning and checked in. While I waited for my turn at the counter, I heard a voice call out my name. Thinking it was my turn, I gathered my purse and stood, only to find a smiling woman facing me.

"Emily, right?"

The smiling woman looked familiar.

"It's me, Kathy. I met you at Iconsiam, at the fashion event?"

"That's right. I remember. I apologize that it took me a moment. I've been a scatterbrain lately."

"Oh, it's quite all right."

"You work here, right?"

"I do. What brings you in today?"

Crap! If I tell her the truth, that will out me. But if I give her some stupid excuse and she finds out it was a lie, it could look bad. Or worst-case scenario, she's the person who would help me file the proper paperwork for my child.

"Um, I'm here to find out about citizenship and how it works."

Kathy immediately glanced down at my tummy. "I didn't know you had a baby. Didn't you just arrive a few months ago?"

"I did. And no, I didn't have a baby yet." I smiled.

"Ah, I got it. Congratulations. Well, I can help you with a Consulate Report for Birth Abroad certificate. No need to wait here in the queue. Follow me."

I sat next to Kathy's desk, and she reviewed the CRBA and what we would need. It was straightforward. She handed me a checklist of all the documents that would be required.

"Do you have any questions?"

"Are there a lot of pregnancies from expats from the States?"

Kathy opened her mouth but then paused, taking a moment to think.

"That many, huh?" I thought maybe she was trying to count.

"The last two that I know of didn't end well. Complications during birth. Both babies were lost. And what made it even worse is that those women gave birth in the same week."

"Oh, no. That's terrible. Did they have their babies at the expat hospital?"

"I believe so."

I won't lie. I breathed a sigh of relief, knowing I had switched to Sasi.

"Do you know the cause or who the OB-GYN was that treated them?"

"No to both of those questions, but I can already see the thoughts running through your head. I don't think you have anything to worry about. The Royal International Hospital has world-class facilities and treatment."

"Did you know those women personally?"

"I knew one. We didn't hang out, but we crossed paths a lot. So, I'd chat with her during those times."

"I see. Um, if I'm overstepping any boundaries, feel free to let me know, but did she mention whether she had complications before birth?"

"I'm not sure about that, but I did talk to her after it happened and recall her mentioning that the loss was unexpected, and the doctor did his best to revive the baby but was unsuccessful."

"What happened to this woman?"

"Her name was Gina Martin. Shortly after giving birth, she and her husband disappeared. The same goes for...oh, what was that other woman's name? I can't remember. Anyway, the same happened to that couple as well."

"They both left Thailand?"

"More like they disappeared. Usually, when someone leaves, there's some farewell party, or everyone finds out ahead of time, so they say goodbye. But not with the Martins or the Dixons. From what I heard, it sounded like the Martins left in the middle of the night. There were no goodbye parties, no 'let's keep-in-touch;' they just disappeared and haven't been heard from again. I'm not clear on the circumstances with the Dixons."

"Oh, my God. That's so freaky."

"Tell me about it."

"Who did you hear this from? You know how rumors can spin out of control. I mean, do you think it's credible?"

"I do, because the sister of my housekeeper worked for the Martins for almost a year. She came into work one day, and the place was empty. All their belongings were gone. The first thought that came to everyone's mind was that they were kidnapped."

"Kidnapped? That happens here?"

"It does. It's a secret that's kept under wraps by the Thai government. People go missing, their bodies are never found, and there is no evidence of them leaving the country. Some of the islands have a long history of it happening."

My jaw just about hit the floor. "Are you serious? Tell me you're pulling my leg."

"I'm serious. But kidnapping was eventually ruled out in the Martins' case because an envelope was left on the counter with her housekeeper's name. It contained her salary. The Martins had taken the time to pay her. So, in the eyes of the local police, that ruled out foul play. If something criminal had happened, there wouldn't have been an envelope. I just think the experience of losing their baby was traumatic, and they wanted out of here quickly."

"I can't believe that happened, but I can see how the death of a newborn could drive a person to act irrationally."

"Of course."

"And the other couple?"

"Gone. They disappeared without a word. They might have planned it together."

"So, there was no investigation?"

"No, because no one could prove a crime had happened. What would the police investigate?"

"I guess you're right about that. Still, it's jarring to hear of people disappearing and cover-ups."

"It happens. By the way, if you're looking for a housekeeper, she's available. I can personally vouch for her."

"You know, I have been thinking about someone who can help around the house and with the baby."

"Well, she was all set to help Gina with her newborn. She's

had two kids herself. They're grown now, so she's got the experience. If you want, I can talk to my housekeeper and get her sister's contact information for you."

"Yes, I would like that. Thank you so much for your help. I appreciate it."

"No problem. And I'm sorry I spooked you with the pregnancies of those other women. That wasn't my intention."

"It's okay. I'm fine. But if I could ask one other favor of you?"

"Sure."

"Could you keep my pregnancy quiet? My husband and I haven't said anything. We are waiting until well after the first trimester before telling people."

"Mum's the word. Good luck."

I left the embassy with so many questions. Two couples both lost their babies at birth within a week of each other and then suddenly disappeared. The chance this was a coincidence was astronomical. More importantly, was this something I needed to worry about?

Chapter Twenty-Six

I HURRIED straight home after I left the embassy. All I wanted to do was get online and dig up any information I could on those couples and the deaths of their babies. I just couldn't accept that two different American women could lose their babies to complications at birth, at the same time, at the same hospital, and then disappear in the middle of the night with no explanation but a shrug. I needed to know if this was hospital-related, doctor-related, or something else, like the air or food. I already knew I was prone to having a difficult pregnancy. I needed to do everything possible to give my baby the best chance at survival.

Of course, there was nothing in the local papers about the babies or the disappearance of the Martins or the Dixons, but why would there be? The deaths of those babies weren't deemed crimes, nor were the disappearances of those couples. It was an unfortunate experience at best. I also found no mention of the Martins or the Dixons in any expat groups on social media. I thought there might be some discussion, considering how the community thrived on gossip, but I came up empty.

Do people here even care what happens to others?

After a few hours, I stopped searching, but my curiosity was still active. I thought briefly of calling Sasi and seeing if she had heard anything about the babies or had colleagues who worked at the expat hospital that knew of the situation.

I continued my search in the expat groups on Facebook, using Gina's name to see if she had even been active. Nothing. But, while poking around, I discovered something unexpected. Kimmy was a moderator for a popular group. Was she also the owner of the group? I'd never suspected she would be involved in that capacity. I looked at the other popular expat group, but the moderator's information wasn't public. On a hunch, I decided to Google Kimmy's name.

A lot of local stuff came up, especially if I looked at the image results. She was listed in many photographs from various events since her arrival in Thailand. Vivian and Jackie were also included in most of those photos, but some were just of Kimmy and other people. As I continued to peruse, I noticed a woman who appeared with Kimmy in many images. She was also in several photos with Vivian and Jackie. One thing made her stand out. She was a foreigner and stood next to Vivian in a few pictures. Vivian always made sure one of us was on either side of her when taking a photo.

Who is this mystery woman?

I searched for an image of her that had names listed and was able to confirm who she was. She was Gina Martin.

Oh, my God! Gina had been a part of the friend group. It was the only reason she would be standing next to Vivian like that in so many of the photos.

So, you also occupied the seat. I guess you had a decent run, because you're in so many photos. Did your disappearance have anything to do with your standing in the group? Was the pregnancy rule in effect during that time? You lost your baby, so you and your husband left Thailand? Hmmm...

I also realized then that Meredith didn't show up with the

girls in any of the photos. Her time in the group must have been a blip. She really didn't make it past the initial vibe check.

Now I know why Meredith constantly brings up the rules; she's needling me for information in hopes that I'm having the same problem. She's merely projecting about the bitter taste left in her mouth from not making the cut.

Gina was in enough photos of the girls that I found it strange that her name was never mentioned during our conversations. If Gina had been a part of the group, one would think her name might have popped up in conversation. It never did. In fact, none of the girls talked about any previous people in the group. It's like they had scrubbed them out of existence. Was that also a rule? No discussing previous members of the group?

The bigger question was whether the pregnancy rule was in play when Gina was a part of the group, and if it was, how did she handle it? Did she ask for permission, or go down the path I had chosen? Or maybe the rule was enacted after she gave birth, or after she left Thailand? At the very least, I now had a face to match the name.

The more I Googled, the more pictures of Gina I found. And if I went back even further in time, I discovered another woman preceded Gina as the fourth group member. Meredith had been right in that regard; my spot had a history of being a revolving seat.

Eventually, I figured out that other woman's name. She was Sheila Chin. Again, I'd never heard her name mentioned before by the group. As far as I knew, there was currently no Sheila Chin in Bangkok. I would have met her by now if she were still around. She must have left Thailand, and I was dying to know the circumstances. Did she have a problem with the girls, or was it something else, like with Gina?

And why couldn't I find any information on those two after they left Thailand? Did they just opt to lead a private life from that moment on? It was possible, but not likely. How do you go from being in the premier friend group to being invisible?

Just then, I got a text from Kathy at the embassy. She had the contact number for the housekeeper. Her name was Natti. I called her immediately and scheduled a meeting for later in the afternoon. Sure, I was interested in hiring a housekeeper who was good with children. I might need the help, but I was more interested in finding out what happened to Gina Martin.

Natti agreed to meet me at the Starbucks near my home. On the walk over to the coffee shop, I knew I was heading down a rabbit hole, but I couldn't stop. My pregnancy was too important to me, and if something had affected those other women, I wanted to know about it. At least, that was the little lie I told myself. When I arrived, I spotted a woman sitting alone inside the coffee shop.

"Are you Natti?" I asked as I approached her.

"Yes, I'm her," she said with a beaming smile.

"I'm Emily. Thank you for meeting me on such short notice. Can I get you a coffee or a tea?"

"No, thank you, I'm fine."

I sat in the seat opposite her. Her eyes never veered from me, nor did her smile diminish. It projected confidence, and I already liked her.

"How do you know Mrs. Kathy?" she asked after I got settled.

"I met her at an event once before and ran into her again today at the embassy. It's such a small world here in Bangkok. The expat community is such a tight-knit group. I guess that's a good thing; it led to our meeting."

"Yes."

I could tell small talk wasn't something Natti was interested in. She probably just wanted the details so she could decide whether to work for me.

"What was it like working for Gina Martin?" I asked.

"Mrs. Gina is a very nice lady. I liked working for her."

"And you aren't currently with another family right now?"

"I don't understand what you asked me," the lines across Natti's forehead deepened.

"I mean, you're not working right now. Is that correct?"

She shook her head. "I'm not working."

I quickly explained my situation to her and when my baby was due. I was honest and told her that I didn't need anyone right then, at least not until we were closer to the baby's due date. I also told her that I'd never hired a nanny or a housekeeper before, so I didn't know anything about protocol or how the work was structured.

"Don't worry, Mrs. Emily. I have been a housekeeper and nanny for a long time. We can change things once we know each other better."

"Oh, that sounds fabulous. I feel so much better, but…" my voice trailed off as I looked away.

"Is there a problem?" she asked with concern.

"I'm probably just being overly cautious." I didn't feel like getting into the details of my past with Natti, since we'd just met. "I have questions that are too early to be asked. But I am interested, especially since you're already a mother, and this will be my first child."

Yes, I lied. But I don't even think it mattered to Natti. I felt that a quarter of what I said went over her head because of the language barrier.

"I'm happy to help. I love children. Mine are big and busy with their families."

"That does happen. Do you have grandchildren?"

She nodded. "I do. My daughter has two children, and they live with me. My son and his family live up north. I watch my grandchildren when my daughter is working."

"Will you be able to help your daughter and me at the same time?"

"Yes, no problem. Don't worry, okay?"

I nodded. "Kathy told me a little about Gina's situation—her loss."

"It was a very sad time for Mrs. Gina. I cried for her. A terrible thing to happen to a kind woman. The burn made things worse."

"Burn? What do you mean by burn?"

"In Thailand, we don't bury people; we burn the body."

"Oh, cremation."

"If you don't give the hospital special instructions, they will burn."

"Wait, Gina was unaware that her child would be cremated without her approval?"

Natti shrugged. "All the hospitals have it listed in the forms you sign. It was a miss, mis…understand."

"Misunderstanding?"

"Yes," Natti said, nodding. "If she told the hospital not to do this, they would keep the body. But it's normal, plus only burn body can be taken out of Thailand."

"That makes sense. I mean, how would they transport the body? Ashes would be the way to go."

"Yes, it's easy to take care of the funeral here."

"Does anybody bury bodies here?"

Natti held up her hand and pinched her forefinger to her thumb. "Little bit."

"What a shock it must have been for them to be told they couldn't see their baby one last time."

I leaned back into my chair, dumbfounded by what I had

learned. It was bad enough that Gina lost her baby, but to be told the body was cremated without her realizing must have amplified everything she felt. You can't come back from a cremation. It's such a final act. I'm sure the hospital followed protocol like they always do. This was, as Natti had said, a misunderstanding. A cultural misunderstanding. Still, if it were me, I'd be pissed and want something done.

"What happened after Gina found out her baby was cremated?"

Natti shrugged. "I don't know."

"I mean, did she try to sue the hospital?"

"Sue for what? She signed the paper. Thailand is not like America. If you think things will work the same way, you will be disappointed." Natti took a short breath as if she were contemplating her next words, but nothing came.

"What is it?" I asked.

"Why do we talk so much about Gina and not the job? Did you know her before?"

"I'm sorry. I didn't know her, but because I'm pregnant, I'm sensitive to anything wrong happening to other women with their babies. Gina wasn't the only expat who lost her baby. Another woman also lost her baby that same week due to problems with the birth."

"I understand now."

"Some people I know were friends with Gina. Did she ever mention the name Vivian Wagner?"

Natti gasped and straightened up in her seat. "Vivian?" She quickly grabbed her purse and stood. "I'm sorry, but I can't work for you."

"Wait, what happened?" I asked, standing and reaching out to stop Natti from walking away. "Was it something I said?"

"Mrs. Vivian makes a lot of trouble for Mrs. Gina. A lot of

stress makes her have problems when she is pregnant. She made Mrs. Gina feel bad about being pregnant."

Hearing those words come from Natti's mouth was like being socked in the stomach. My worst fear had materialized. The pregnancy rule was real—and enforced.

"Natti, did Vivian do something to Gina?"

"She became very stressed and sick. I think this is what caused the problems and why Mrs. Gina loses the baby."

"What else did Gina say about Vivian? Did she say anything about rules? Did she say anything about needing permission to be pregnant?"

"Just stay away from Mrs. Vivian." Natti glanced at my belly. "Think about your child."

"Don't leave just yet. I have so many questions."

Natti wrestled her arm out of my grip. "I'm sorry, I must go. I don't want anything to do with that woman. She's dangerous."

"How so? You must tell me."

"I'm sorry. I don't want to be seen talking to you."

Natti left the Starbucks quickly, leaving me wondering what I had gotten myself into with the group.

Chapter Twenty-Seven

I HURRIED BACK HOME, opened my laptop, and threw myself into a deep dive on Vivian and Kip Wagner. I wanted to know who these people were, where they came from, and whether they had a hidden past. I saw no reason for Natti to benefit from spreading false rumors about Vivian. She seemed genuinely scared of the woman and was even afraid to say more. I highly doubted she was putting on a show. What would be the reason? She needed a job. She could have had one with me. Why would she throw that opportunity away? Was it to be vindictive toward Vivian for what happened to Gina? I wasn't buying the logic. It was too much effort for so little benefit.

For the next hour or so, I did my best to learn all I could about the Wagners. It wasn't that difficult to find surface-level stuff on Vivian because of all the functions she attended. But if I wanted real information about her, that was hard to come by. She didn't have a Facebook account. She had a presence on Instagram, but it was merely an extension of the Vivian brand. She favored text messages over messaging apps. I always figured she was "old school" in those respects.

The Friend Group

With all the time we spent together since my arrival, you'd think I would know a lot about her. However, the more I thought about it, the more I realized I had gotten to know a very curated version of Vivian. As for her husband, Kip, he was even more elusive. Aside from a LinkedIn profile, I couldn't find anything on the guy.

I wished I'd mentioned Jackie and Kimmy to Natti. Whatever was going on could involve all three women. I knew Jackie and Kimmy had Facebook accounts, because I was friends with them. But their other connections were mostly family and friends. Their Instagram accounts were very much like Vivian's. It was how they communicated with the public.

I looked closer at Jackie's and Kimmy's posts to learn more about Vivian. I knew they had both arrived in Bangkok about two years ago, and gauging from their posts, it seemed like they both met Vivian shortly after their arrival. I didn't find it strange, as their husbands worked for Kip, just like Jake. Vivian probably reached out to them.

While looking through Jackie's old posts, I found one that had a picture of her, Vivian, and Gina. I would have thought there would be more, because there were a lot of posts with me. In fact, looking through Kimmy's social media, I found no photos of Gina. But I knew Gina had been a member of the group at one point. Did they scrub their social media of anything having to do with Gina? It certainly looked like it. All the other pictures I found of Gina and the three were posted by the hosting organizations of those events.

Wait, what are you doing, Emily? Why are you playing investigative journalist with your friends?

I leaned back in my chair, thinking it had to be my overactive imagination at work. It had to be the other side of me, the one I sometimes had trouble controlling.

Suddenly, I broke into tears. I wanted to believe I could control my thoughts because I could go months at a time, keeping myself in check. I knew the difference between reality and my imagination. I had even controlled it well enough to have my therapist sign off on my stability. I wept into my hands, fearful that if Jake were to find out about my relapsing, our marriage might not survive it this time. I was scared to death of bringing a child into the world knowing my condition. Would Jake divorce me and fight for custody by claiming I was unfit to be a mother?

I grabbed a box of tissues and wiped my tears away.

Get a grip on yourself, Emily. You're not damaged. You know what's real and what's not. You know it's perfectly normal for people to talk to themselves. We pose questions and then proceed to answer them. Everyone does it. But people almost always give the answer they want to hear.

My therapist had made that argument on numerous occasions. What she said made complete sense. The issue that made me susceptible to believing my own arguments was a lack of confidence in myself. I was insecure and often thought the worst was all I was good enough for. For years I had been my own worst enemy. Dr. Young helped me realize I was better. And it worked enough for me to recognize when I would relapse into my old behavior and correct it. I had everyone fooled.

Now I was in Bangkok, relapsing into my old ways where I would make up fabulous stories about people that became truths in my narrative. I couldn't allow that to happen again.

"You are strong. You are intelligent. You are normal," I said, voicing my affirmations out loud.

There had to be a good reason for Natti's behavior and accusations toward Vivian. And if there wasn't, well, then it was only my time lost. The way I saw things, my unborn child mattered most. If this was all an exercise in rumors and cattiness, fine. But if something truly sinister had happened, then it was my duty to find out what that was. That was my job, to look out for my child and myself. Rules or no rules, I was not about to lose this baby.

Chapter Twenty-Eight

I DID my best to ignore my thoughts for the next few days. I wanted to see what a few clear days would do to my mindset and my thoughts on what Natti had told me. During that time, I had dinner with the girls, and everything was fine, though I would still catch Vivian eyeing me. Jackie, Kimmy, and I could all be laughing, and Vivian would sit there quietly, never taking her gaze off me. Was she still unsure about my status in the group, or was it something else, like knowing I was pregnant?

While I was walking on the treadmill in the complex's gym, my mind wandered. I began taking stock of everything I had learned that played a role in pushing me to that dark space a few days ago. This included Vivian and the girls, the rules, my conversation with Natti, her accusations about Vivian, Gina's time in the group, and finally, Gina and the Dixon woman losing their babies in the same week. It was a lot to take stock of, but I had every intention of taking a neutral, methodical approach to all that information.

My Friend Group

The Friend Group

As friends, Vivian, Jackie, and Kimmy were fantastic and amazingly loyal. They did nothing but welcome me into their lives and helped me successfully navigate my life in Bangkok. Not only that, but they also gave me access to a life I could only have dreamed of before I met them. The network that I had been able to develop would serve me well, even if Jake and I chose to leave Bangkok. There was no way I could repay the generosity the girls had shown to me.

But Vivian was strange in her ways, and I admit she frightened me when we first met. She was intimidating and came across as cold. But once I got to know her, those feelings mostly disappeared. She was very private and spoke little about her past or her relationship with Kip. Vivian would rather sit quietly and listen to what others were saying. She was diplomatic and friendly enough for people to gravitate toward her. You don't develop her reputation without being likable. Vivian didn't derive her power from wealth, or from a company or government position, like many in Bangkok did. She wasn't from an influential family, nor was she married to a man of great power outside his company. Yet, she moved in that circle with relative ease and comfort.

My initial thought was that she knew about people's skeletons. But her sway wasn't just with a few individuals but with everyone she encountered. With someone that powerful, it's better to be on her good side. So why was I desperately wanting to rock the boat with her?

The Rules

No matter what we do or face in life, there will be limitations to what we can and cannot do. Rules are a fact of life. They keep society somewhat in control. They're usually put into place for a good reason. And if they're followed, the outcome is generally favorable. Was there something really that bad about the rules for the friend group? Not in the big scheme of things. I think most friends abide by most of these rules to some degree without having to etch them into stone. It's a given. The pregnancy rule would throw anyone for a loop. And no outside friends would be a close second. I never did get clarification. What I did instead was provide an answer to myself instead of clarifying further what Vivian meant about permission.

Natti the Housekeeper

I had just met the woman. I knew very little about her, but I had latched on to every accusation she uttered because I wanted to be right about Vivian. I didn't want to be caught lacking like I had with Noah. Some days, I still felt like Noah would be with me today if I had been more proactive, more watchful, more everything. On the flip side, it wasn't fair to Vivian to accuse, judge, and penalize her, all inside my head, without hearing her side of the story. Aside from being a stickler for rules, what had she done to me? I could flip the script on Natti and investigate what axe she could have to grind.

Gina Martin

She lost her baby, and I was sorry that happened to her. I knew how she must have felt; I knew what she went through. I completely understood her wanting to take herself out of this place. Bangkok had probably come to represent pain and resentment. For her, it will always be the place where she lost her baby. And she will always wonder if it was preventable. I, for one, did not want the same thing to happen to my baby. I stood by my decision to switch to Sasi. The underlying cause of

Gina's baby's death was unknown to me. Could Gina really have had that much stress in her life that it made her pregnancy dangerous? It was plausible, but I had no proof that was what happened. And if stress was the cause, did Vivian really play a role, and was it intentional?

The Dixons

I knew very little about them, except they had lost their baby the same week and at the same hospital as Gina. Was there a connection? Did they have the same doctor? As with Gina, I understood wanting to flee from Thailand. Had the same happened to me, I would want out of this place. Would I leave the same way, in the middle of the night? Maybe, it's hard to tell. The hiccup I had was the coincidental timing. I mean, what were the odds? It seemed highly unlikely. The expat hospital was well known and treated thousands of people from all over the world.

I stepped off the treadmill, raising my arms over my head for a long stretch. All that examination of what I had learned didn't produce a smoking gun or answer to settle all my questions and concerns. It told me that the attention I gave to these topics stemmed from wanting to protect my unborn child. It was nothing more than vigilance. What mother-to-be wouldn't want a natural trait like that, primarily if it could save her children? I had past mistakes to learn from.

That day on the treadmill, I made a promise to myself. My child would come first. I would prioritize nothing over having a healthy pregnancy. If I had to lose friends and status for that to happen, then so be it. I was not about to make the same mistake I made with Noah. I would not assume everything would be okay. This time, I planned on embracing another side of me: the side that saw the evil in people.

Chapter Twenty-Nine

EVEN THOUGH I had developed a plan to keep my pregnancy on track, I felt like I needed a confidant. Jake was that person in every way, except with matters like the one I was currently dealing with. The trouble I had recovering from Noah's death had rocked our marriage like nothing before. Janice thought it made my relationship with Jake stronger, that making it through something like that would prepare us for even more significant challenges, should they come. And to some degree, she was right. It's just that I'd always had the feeling Jake was looking for signs of relapse. He thought I'd stopped therapy way too early. He suggested I continue, but maybe not as frequently. He even told me to talk to someone here in Bangkok, fearing the move might trigger something inside me. There was nothing to trigger, nothing to relapse to. I hadn't suddenly become cured. I learned to manage my thoughts. That's all.

There was one person I thought I could turn to and trust during this period.

"Hi, Emily," Sasi said as she entered the small coffee shop where we'd become accustomed to meeting. Lately, she'd been busier at her practice, and we'd had to meet at night, which was fine by me. It left my days free to mingle with the girls and avoid the alcohol-fueled events at night.

"Hi, Sasi. Did you have a busy day?"

"Busy but not regretful. I got to reveal the sex of a baby to a patient today. It never gets old, seeing the look on their faces. Speaking of, have you made up your mind?"

During my last ultrasound, Sasi was able to determine the sex of my child and asked if I wanted to know. I was suddenly terrified to find out, and I couldn't explain why. Maybe it was because doing so would remind me that I could have had two sons or a son and a daughter. I had told Sasi to hold off and that I would let her know when I was ready.

She didn't seem bothered by it and said it wasn't uncommon for mothers-to-be to want to wait a little longer or not know at all and wait for the surprise later.

"I think I'm ready," I said.

"Are you sure?"

"I am. Tell me, please."

"It's a boy."

"A boy?"

My eyes welled, and a second later, I was dabbing with a tissue.

"I'm sorry," I said as I sniffed. "I can't believe I'm having a boy."

Sasi leaned across the table and gave me a hug. "You are, and he'll be perfect, just like his mother."

"He will, won't he?"

"Of course."

"Thank you, Sasi."

"For what? I'm just doing my job."

I couldn't control my tears as they continued to rain down. They were tears of joy, but somewhere in there, a few tears of sadness mixed in. I should have been telling Noah that he would soon have a little brother.

"I can't believe I'm having a boy. Jake will be thrilled."

Sasi grabbed hold of my hand and gave it a gentle squeeze. "I'm very happy for you two, and I can't wait to meet your son."

Later that night, I patiently waited for Jake to return home. I kept standing, sitting, and standing again, looking out from the balcony, unable to contain my excitement. I had a bottle of sparkling cider for us to celebrate with. Jake had made it no secret that he wanted a son. Sure, he would have been happy with a daughter. But he wanted a son and joked we'd keep trying until he got one. I finally heard the door unlock, and in walked Jake.

"Hi," I said, throwing my arms around him and kissing him.

"Hello to you, too. You're looking a little feisty."

"Well, maybe I am." I loosened his tie.

"I like where this is going."

"You'll have to wait a little while longer."

I poured the cider into two glasses and handed him one.

"I have something exciting to tell you," I said.

"Did we win the Thai lottery?"

"Not quite, but we did get a win. I found out about the sex of our baby today. We're having a boy."

"For real? Whoo-hoo! This is the best news ever." Jake wrapped me up in his arms and hugged me tightly as he spun me around. "This is amazing news. Are you happy with a boy?" He looked at me with bright eyes full of joy.

"Of course. I would be happy with either sex."

Jake touched his forehead against mine and looked into my eyes. He had that look that I loved. The one that made me so happy with him. He was a man who was deeply in love with me, that I knew for sure. At that moment, all I wanted was for him to take me into the bedroom and make love to me.

Jake lowered me back to the floor before taking a seat on the couch. He still looked like he was in a state of shock as he absorbed the news. His eyes seemed vacant, but his smile told a different story. He leaned back into the couch, clasping his hands behind his head. "I can't believe we're having a boy. I can't wait. I really can't wait."

By the look on his face, I had a good idea of what he was thinking. Jake had played basketball since he was a little boy and went as far as playing for a top university, but a knee injury ended his basketball career. Jake was tall (six feet four inches) and muscular. He would show me video clips of him playing in college. He was a force to be reckoned with as he would muscle his way toward the net and dunk the ball.

I was a shrimp compared to him, standing only five feet four inches. Our son's height could go either way. But I knew Jake wouldn't be deterred by that. I could see it now: a basketball in the crib and a basketball-themed mobile hanging above. He had done it with Noah. Basketball outfits were a given, and as soon as he could take a step, Jake would have him on the court.

I sat on the couch, scooting up against him so he could put an arm around me. "Are you happy?" I asked again.

"I'm thrilled. We will finally start the family we were meant to have."

I didn't want to spoil the moment for Jake, but I knew things were far from perfect. I had my own issues to deal with, primarily keeping my stress levels low and my health optimal. I wanted everything to be perfect for our family. We deserved to be happy. I wanted Jake to be a proud father and me a doting mother. But for that to happen, certain people needed to be dealt with, meaning Vivian.

Chapter Thirty

WITH JAKE UP TO speed with the pregnancy, the next step was shopping. I had no plans with the girls, so I was free to shop all day. I knew the places I wanted to go; most were away from areas where Vivian and the others might be. But there was that one baby boutique near Vivian's favorite place to lunch. It was risky to shop there, but it had the cutest outfits, and if I recalled correctly, they had basketball outfits that would be perfect.

The shopping center opened at ten. The odds of Vivian, Jackie, or Kimmy being there that early were slim to none. I figured I would make that my first stop and limit myself to an hour.

When I arrived at the shopping center, I had about a five-minute wait before the doors were opened and people were allowed in. I made a beeline straight to the shop. It was empty when I arrived, and I breathed a sigh of relief. It wasn't just Vivian, Jackie, and Kimmy I had to worry about. Anyone in the expat community could be a potential threat. Gossip moved fast in the city.

I slipped inside the store, and the shopgirl greeted me immediately. She was young, under twenty-five. I wasn't worried about her opening her mouth. Underneath that false smile was a person who wanted nothing more than to be someplace else.

"How may I help you?" she asked.

"I saw a basketball outfit in the display window the last time I was here, but I don't see it now."

"We moved it to the back."

I lost track of time as I got caught up in picking out outfits. By the time the shopgirl finished ringing me up, it was nearly 11:30. I'd have to hurry out of the area to avoid being seen. The bags alone were a huge giveaway.

Before leaving the shop, I gave the place a cursory glance. I didn't see anyone familiar, so I made my move. I walked quickly toward the exit, keeping my head down and avoiding eye contact. As I approached the doorway, I glanced back over my shoulder—for no real reason except to assure myself that I hadn't been seen.

Behind me was a group of Japanese tourists. Just as I was about to heave a sigh of relief, I spotted her: Vivian was standing outside a shop and looking directly at me.

No!

It was brief, as the crowd of tourists obscured my view immediately after I saw her. I craned my neck, and after a few seconds, my line of sight opened, but Vivian was gone.

I quickly searched for her, thinking she was on a fast approach in my direction, but I didn't see her. Could I have been mistaken? Was it just someone who looked like Vivian?

My therapist once mentioned that if I saw something only briefly, it was possible that it wasn't there and was a figment of my imagination. She'd said it was a good way to separate fiction from reality. I always tried to remember that, and it seemed to work. Since Vivian was no longer there, it had to be my mind playing tricks on me.

I hurried toward the rank of taxis. Once safely inside the

car, I looked back at the mall entrance. I still didn't see Vivian. My phone pinged right then. It was Vivian. She'd said hello through a GIF to the group chat. It was common for us to do this, so there was no reason to think it was anything but that. Except I wasn't sure if she'd seen me or not.

It was six in the evening by the time I got back home. I'd had two more Vivian sightings. I knew deep down inside there was no way she would have any reason to shop where I was. Vivian was very picky about where she shopped. She told me once that it was important for us to keep our standards up when out and about by ourselves. "Don't give anyone any reason to start something with you, because there are women here who will," she'd always say to us. Vivian curated her brand daily, and it paid off for her. She had power in Bangkok, even with the Thais. I would never want to be on her bad side.

But I was pregnant.

Those other sightings were brief—seconds, really. I also dubbed them figments of my imagination. I ran through the checklist my therapist had given me after each sighting of Vivian.

Was what I saw brief or unclear? Yes.

Was there any interaction with what I saw? No.

I'd answered honestly and therefore ruled out the Vivian sightings as real. I was confident no one had seen me and forgot about it.

When Jake walked through the front door, I grabbed him by the hand and led him to the room we had deemed the nursery.

"What's going on?" he asked as I led him down the hallway.

"I went shopping today. Wait until you see what I bought!"

Jake stopped at the bedroom doorway. "Wow, that's a lot of shopping bags."

"I know. I haven't put them away because I'm waiting for the perfect dresser to arrive. I ordered it online."

I dug into a bag and pulled out the basketball outfit. "Ta-da!"

"This is so cool. My little basketball player. I can't wait to see him in it." Jake's brow crinkled a tad bit. "But why did you buy the identical outfit in a larger size? Is this for when he's older?"

"No, silly, that's for Noah, so they can match."

Later that night, I woke to find Jake's side of the bed empty, and he wasn't in the bathroom. I slipped out of bed and made my way out to the living room. The lights were off; however, the door to his office was cracked, and a sliver of light showed. As I tiptoed my way there, I could hear a hushed conversation, which I thought was strange. Why would Jake be having a meeting this late at night? It was after two in the morning.

I stopped near the doorway. He was talking to someone, and it was a woman. I couldn't quite make out what they were talking about, so I moved closer until I could see through the cracked opening. Jake was sitting at his desk facing the window, so his back was to me. He was on a video call, but his head was blocking the person on the call.

"I'm worried," he said. "It's not the first instance."

Worried? What is he talking about?

"What I want you to do is keep documenting it every time it happens," the woman said.

When what happens?

"Do you think you should talk to her?" Jake asked.

Is Jake talking about me?

"It would probably be better if she sees someone there."

That voice, why does it sound familiar?

Jake shifted his body, allowing me to see who he was talking to. It was Dr. Young, my old therapist.

"I'm worried that she's regressing, and with the baby, it'll only get worse. She bought outfits for Noah today," said Jake with worry in his voice.

"But you also said she realized Noah was no longer with you."

"That's correct, she seemed to snap back into reality right at that moment, but she'd gone the whole day thinking she bought matching outfits for the baby and Noah."

"I know this can be concerning, but because Emily was able to determine on her own what was real and what wasn't, I don't think we need to sound the alarm. But it wouldn't hurt for her to talk to someone there. I can make a few calls and recommend someone if you want."

"Yes, please do that. I appreciate you taking the call. I realize you can't discuss anything regarding your sessions with Emily, but bouncing this off you is reassuring."

"You're welcome."

Jake ended the call, and I quickly hurried back to our bedroom and crawled back into bed. A few seconds later, Jake returned and got into bed. I thought briefly about confronting him but decided against it. It would just turn into an argument about me snooping. I couldn't help but wonder how long he'd felt this way. Surely, over the years, I'd had my moments in front of him, but he gave me no indication that he thought I needed to go back to therapy. He always supported and believed in me. Had things changed? Was Jake having doubts? And if so, was he right? Was I going mad again?

Chapter Thirty-One

DEPRESSION RULED THE FOLLOWING DAY. I was so bothered by what I'd heard and seen that I remained in bed until well past noon. Vivian, Jackie, and Kimmy had all messaged me, but I hadn't answered them. In fact, I didn't even read what they had written. I just couldn't shake the thought that Jake might not have my back unconditionally. He was the one person who shouldn't give up on me—through thick and thin. That's what he had vowed to do the day we married.

When I finally crawled out of bed and had a cup of coffee inside me, I read through my messages. Since Christmas was coming up, an organization was having a Toys for Tots drive, and Vivian wanted us all to participate. It was geared toward less fortunate Thai families. My initial thought was yes, I want to help. But there was one other thing that Vivian said that caught my eye. It was strange because she said if we were donating items not to give toys for newborns. They should be for children two and up.

Why two or up? What's the big deal?

But that wasn't all she wrote. She made it a point to direct that comment at me. Did she know about my pregnancy, and was this her passive-aggressive way of tormenting me? Did they all know and decide to play dumb?

Maybe I wasn't imagining Vivian following me. But why would she, anyway? She'd need a reason. How could she have found out? Only four people knew I was pregnant: Jake, Sasi, Natti, and Kathy from the embassy.

Natti knew Vivian, but from what I gathered, she despised her. What reason would she have to say something, unless she said something to someone else and word spread that way? It was possible. I was positive Sasi hadn't said anything, and anyway, she wasn't a part of that crowd. Of course, Jake and I were on the same page. We would remain quiet about the pregnancy until we felt comfortable telling people. Even our parents were unaware. As for Kathy, I didn't know her well enough to peg her as the leak, but I didn't get the impression she was the chatty type like Meredith. There was one other possibility: Vivian could have had her suspicions and been digging ever since. She did ask once if I was pregnant.

But sharing the news about my pregnancy was the least of my problems. My main concern was relapsing and how that would affect my relationship with Jake. It still hurt to discover he thought I was regressing, but we needed to address it. Our lack of communication was part of the problem we faced after Noah died. Avoiding the hard conversations had just made things worse, and I didn't want that to happen this time. We had a fresh start in Bangkok with a solid relationship. And now I was pregnant. We had all the ingredients to start a family, and we both wanted this badly.

Was I going to let this friend group spoil it?

I took a long, hard think about my choices and decisions over the last few weeks. Clearly, I'd given the friend group way more importance than it needed. Sure, the girls were my besties. Sure, I could count on them to be there for me. Sure, they'd done a lot to make me feel welcome. The list went on, but were they more important than Jake, the baby, and me?

No.

And that was the truth. I had to put my family first, and the girls needed to be secondary, at least until I got through the pregnancy. All my stress and overthinking derived from the group. Jake had always told me not to overthink the so-called rules. He was right. I had made a mountain out of a molehill. They weren't really rules. When you visit a friend's home, you don't put your feet up on the coffee table. It's a given, an understanding. Right?

But could I honestly treat Vivian's rules that way?

Those images of her staring me down were burned into my mind. Was that me making it an issue? Was I the problem? I thought not.

I popped up off the couch and walked to the soon-to-be nursery. I stared into the bedroom, imagining the crib all set up and our baby boy cooing as he reached up at the mobile. That was what I wanted. I needed to protect my child at all costs. If it cost me my friendship with the girls, then so be it.

Chapter Thirty-Two

Sasi called and invited me to join her for coffee. It was a welcome relief from sitting alone in the apartment. She suggested a place I hadn't been to, in a neighborhood I wasn't familiar with, saying I would get a kick out of this place. Whether I did or not, it was an excuse to get out of the apartment.

When I arrived at the coffee shop, my first impression was "wow." The outside resembled a large tree, and the shop was tucked into a tree hollow. I could see Sasi inside, and she'd already ordered my usual drink.

"Hi, Emily," Sasi said as soon as I entered.

"Hi, Sasi." I took a seat opposite her. "This place is so cute."

The interior was designed to look like the inside of a tree, with wooden floors and walls carved and shaped to look like a hollow oak tree. The ceiling was painted sky blue, and leaves and vines crawled up the walls. The seating area had these cute little booths that resembled tiny nooks in a tree. There were also squirrel-themed murals and acorn-shaped lamps hanging from the ceiling. The name of the place was simple: Oak.

"Isn't it neat? I saw an article on it and have wanted to come here ever since. I hope the distance wasn't too much of a problem for you."

I waved off her concern. "No problem at all."

"How are you feeling?" Sasi asked. I sensed concern in her voice.

"Fine. I've been doing my best to keep stress out of my life. I exercise in the mornings. I'm eating healthy."

"Good to hear it. So, no problems in the social arena?"

"If you're asking about not drinking at the events I attend, then no. So far, I've been able to get away with it with some nifty tricks I developed." I patted my tummy gently. "But I am starting to show."

"Yes, well, there's no stopping that, but I was asking about your friends, not so much the alcohol. I'm assuming you haven't told them yet?"

"Jake and I haven't told anyone."

"Okay, well, I'm happy to hear all of this. I've always told you that your physical health is important for the pregnancy, but your mental health is equally important."

"I know..." I said, letting my voice trail off.

"I've known you long enough to know that look on your face. What is it?"

I thought briefly about my past with Sasi. Until then, I had cherry-picked and told her only what I thought necessary. But being that she was officially my OB-GYN and a good friend, it made sense to bring her into the fold.

"There is something I do want to share with you."

"Yes, share. I'm all ears."

"I used to see a therapist."

Sasi shrugged. "Okay, so? Is that the big secret? Because it's not a big deal."

"I know, but the reason for therapy might be off the beaten path."

I explained to her how difficult it had been to deal with Noah's death and that I had grief hallucinations that confused reality with my imagination. She sat quietly and listened, occasionally nodding, never giving me any indication that she was judging me. I felt good about that.

"But I'm okay now. I won't say I'm one hundred percent 'over' Noah's death, but I can manage my feelings about it."

"Emily, everything you told me is perfectly normal. To have a child and then lose it months later is traumatic."

"I know, I know. It's just that sometimes I still have those thoughts. The other day I went shopping for the baby, and I ended up buying matching outfits. One for the baby and one for Noah. It wasn't until I got home and showed Jake what I'd purchased that it dawned on me. Literally, as those words were coming out of my mouth, I snapped out of it. I'm worried I'm relapsing. I'm worried this will cause stress. I'm worried my mental health will jeopardize the pregnancy."

Sasi reached across the table and took my hand. "Listen, Emily. These thoughts you're having are normal. We all deal with grief in different ways. There is no time limit, either. In fact, there is no rule stating you must stop grieving. What is important is that you can manage your thoughts and feelings. This tells me you're in control."

"But what if—"

"No what-ifs. Emily, you're in control. No one else. I know you're concerned with your other friends and this so-called rule about obtaining permission for a pregnancy... Don't even get me started on that ridiculousness. The point I'm trying to make is that you need to prioritize. You and the baby are number one. Your friends will have to take a back seat. And if they can't understand that, then, well, what kind of friends are they?"

"That's exactly what I told myself this morning. But...late last night, I overheard Jake on a video call. He was talking to my

The Friend Group

old therapist about my relapsing. When I was at my worst, our marriage was rocky. The 'D' word had been mentioned. So, you can see why this video call concerns me. He must think I'm going nuts again, or else why would he call?"

"Jake's worried about you. That's why he made the call. Men are natural problem solvers. Fixing things is how they cope. Jake sees a problem and gets into that mindset where he believes it's his responsibility to make things right. That video call was his way of trying to take care of you. What I would find troubling is if he did nothing. That would tell me he didn't care. But you see, that's not what happened."

I let out a breath. "You're right, as usual. Talking with you always puts things into the right perspective."

"I'm not only your friend but also your doctor. It's my job to make sure you get through the pregnancy without any problems. My only goal here is to place a healthy baby boy into your arms." Sasi smiled and winked one of her comforting brown eyes.

"Thank you so much. I'm so glad I met you."

About an hour later, Sasi and I parted company and headed in opposite directions. She had a home visit she needed to make in the neighborhood. I walked slowly, keeping an eye out for a taxi. They were abundant, but each one passing by already had customers. I was about to pull out my phone and book a car on a ride-share app when I spotted a familiar hairdo on a woman across the street. It was Vivian.

I knew her well enough to recognize her from behind: that shape, those clothes, it was definitely her. But what was she doing in this neighborhood? The area was populated with low- to middle-income Thai people—very few foreigners lived there.

What business could she possibly have here? Was she following me? Did she see me with Sasi?

My mind raced for answers as to why I was having coffee with someone outside the group and in this area. I couldn't tell Vivian that Sasi was my OB-GYN; that would give away my pregnancy. If I said Sasi was just an acquaintance I bumped into in passing, that would make her feel bad. As I racked my brain for excuses, it dawned on me that Vivian also had some explaining to do.

That's it. I'll flip the script, go on the offensive, and grill her on why she's here.

Vivian's attention was focused on a building's entranceway, a wooden door that opened inward, revealing a dark space. I stepped behind a small tree growing from the sidewalk in case she turned in my direction. The building was five floors tall, and nearly every one of the front-facing balconies was lined with laundry drying. The exterior of the building was weathered and decrepit, with faded paint peeling in places. I swear some of the cracked windows were staring back at me, making me feel like Vivian had eyes in the back of her head. The ground floor on either side of the doorway was occupied by two mom-and-pop shops.

From what I could tell, it looked like she was talking to someone inside the entranceway. A second later, two men stepped out into the open. They were dressed casually in jeans and T-shirts. Tattoos covered both men's arms, and they had intimidating looks on their faces. Their shifty eyes kept watch on street and sidewalk. Were they worried about being seen, or were they worried about unexpected guests?

Is Vivian in trouble?

I didn't recognize the men, but she could have easily walked away if she was in trouble. They weren't physically detaining her. In fact, from where I stood, the three looked to be engaged in a conversation.

My first thought was that these men might have been two of the many security guards hired to work the events we attended, but why would Vivian come all the way over here to have a conversation with them?

Just then, Vivian removed what looked like an envelope from her purse and handed it over. The larger of the two snatched it away, opened it, and briefly removed a wad of cash before shoving it back in.

Now, I'd been in Bangkok long enough to know it wasn't a good thing when you handed over cash stuffed inside an envelope. It was so easy to make an instant bank transfer if you were paying for services, buying goods, or even lending money. Cash was untraceable. Cash in an envelope was sketchy.

Vivian glanced back over both shoulders. She had a serious look on her face, not one of fear. Some agreed-upon business was taking place. She had a few more words with the men before hurrying off. The two men retreated into the building.

So that's interesting. Vivian sneaks around. And this time, there was no confusion about whether I imagined it. She was there. It was all real.

Was Vivian harboring secrets? Certainly, that was against the rules. I couldn't help but think I might have stumbled across leverage. Imagine that? Something I could hold over Vivian's head.

Chapter Thirty-Three

During my ride home in the taxi, I thought about all the logical reasons why Vivian would hand over an envelope stuffed with cash to two men who looked like gangsters. No way she was there to spy on me.

Was Vivian in debt?

Did her husband have a gambling problem, and she was forced to deal with it?

Or worse, was Vivian in serious trouble, and no one, not even her husband, was aware of it?

The taxi stopped at the gated entrance to the property, next to the guard shack. Sometimes the taxis don't like driving inside, because it's a hassle for them. I paid the fare and collected my purse.

"Good afternoon, Ms. Emily." Pai, the security guard, had hurried over to hold the car door open for me.

"Hi, Pai. How are you today?"

"I'm good." He had that familiar smile on his face that said he hadn't a worry in the world. I wished I could be more like him. I was sure he didn't spend his days dreaming up problems to solve.

"Congratulations," he said.

I gave him a curious look and then saw that he had glanced at my tummy. My dress had shifted around my midsection and showed off my tiny bump.

"Thank you, Pai." I pressed a finger against my lips. "Let's keep this a secret, okay?"

"Mr. Jake don't know you are pregnant?"

I chuckled. "He knows, but we haven't told anyone yet."

He nodded. "Good idea. It's safer this way."

"Safer? What do you mean?" I asked as I choked on my words.

"It's nothing." He waved off my question and started walking back to the guard shack.

"No, wait, Pai. Why is it safer to keep it a secret? Please tell me."

Pai looked around as he swallowed. His demeanor went from happy-go-lucky to one of concern and uneasiness.

"Pai, is everything okay? Are you in trouble?"

"No, no. I'm fine, but you must be careful." He pointed to my belly.

"Why? What do you know?"

"Take care of your baby. Make sure it's healthy. Don't let anyone take you after you give birth."

Did Pai know about the other women who lost their babies? If they lived in the complex, I supposed he would.

"Pai, did you know Gina Martin?"

"Yes, I know Ms. Gina. She was so sad about her baby. This why, I tell you."

"You think my baby will die after I give birth like her baby?"

"Her baby not die."

"Are you sure we're talking about the same person? Gina Martin."

"Yes, I know Ms. Gina, but her baby did not die."

Pai shifted his weight from one foot to the other and continuously looked around as if he were afraid of being seen talking to me.

"If her baby didn't die, then what happened, Pai? I need to know to keep my baby safe. Did Gina and Vivian have a problem?"

Pai looked around once more. "Her baby taken. Not die."

"Taken? Do you mean her baby was kidnapped?"

He nodded. "Sell," he whispered.

"Wait, Pai. I need to be clear on what you're saying here. You're telling me her baby was taken and sold? Do you know the word 'adoption'?"

"Yes, I know. But that did not happen. I'm sorry, Ms. Emily. It's dangerous for me to talk to you about this."

Before I could spit out another question, Pai hurried back into his shack and shut the door. He wouldn't look at me and kept his head down, focused on the papers spread across the desk.

Sold? It couldn't be what he was saying. He must have been confused with the words; he had to have meant adoption. But Natti said Gina lost her baby at birth. Why would she tell me that if it wasn't true?

I knocked on the door to the shack. Pai continued to ignore me, but I continued to rap my knuckles against the window.

He slid the window open. "I'm sorry, Ms. Emily. Forget what I said."

"Pai, do you know Natti? She was Gina's housekeeper."

Pai swallowed hard. That alone told me he did.

"Natti said Gina's baby died after birth. Is that true, Pai? I need to know. You don't want anything to happen to my baby, do you?"

He shook his head. "That's all I know. It's what I hear. Maybe it's not true."

"Pai, I think you know more than you are telling me. Did Vivian have anything to do with this?"

Pai slammed the window shut and pretended I wasn't there.

Chapter Thirty-Four

EVER SINCE I was a little girl, I've been told that I overthink things and have a wild imagination. I don't disagree with that, but it wasn't much of a problem until Noah died. That's when I started acting on the voices in my head. And that's why Jake had pushed me hard to go to therapy. I'd done a pretty good job of hiding that side of me when I first met Jake. Really, there was no reason to tell him I always had these thoughts. What good would it do?

When I started imagining Noah was alive, he thought I was having trouble dealing with his death. And I was, but he eventually learned that I had always been that way. Noah's death revealed it for him.

My therapist had told me that I should be honest with Jake, especially since Noah's death was devastating for both him and me. So, I told Jake. I told him everything and didn't sugarcoat it. He said he loved me and would stand by me. But there were times when I thought he might give up.

But if I were having a total relapse, I'm not sure how Jake would handle it. He didn't even know the truth and was already on the phone with my old therapist. I wasn't one hundred percent sure he would believe my new theory that something strange was happening with the births by expat women, and that Vivian might have something to do with it.

Seeing Pai shut down the way Natti did was telling. Did the Martins and the Dixons lose their babies after birth, or was something being covered up?

If I was wrong about the babies being abducted, what I feared was happening was that I was losing my marbles and needed serious help. What man wants to be married to a woman who can't tell the difference between her imagination and reality? More so, who would want that woman taking care of their child? I'd already lost one. Would Jake think there was a chance it would happen again?

But if I was right...

I entered my apartment, locked the door behind me, and walked straight into my bedroom, flopping onto my bed in tears. Nothing made sense, but at the same time, it seemed like everything did. Talking to Pai had only added to the teetering stack of problems in front of me. Telling Vivian and the others that I was pregnant seemed like nothing compared to the idea of a plot to kidnap expat babies. I rolled over onto my back and wiped my eyes with my hand.

Think this through, Emily. Pai never mentioned the word "kidnapped." However, he did say "taken" and "sold," which is trafficking. Oh, God. It sounds even worse.

Pai might have confused his words. English wasn't his first language. Oh, who was I kidding? He said Gina's baby didn't die. It was stolen and then sold on the black market. I had no proof of that happening, but he and Natti were fearful of Vivian. Was Vivian involved in this? Was there some sort of falling out when Vivian discovered Gina's pregnancy? Surely Vivian had nothing to do with Gina's baby dying. But, if there was any truth to what Pai said, did Vivian orchestrate trafficking?

You're losing it, Emily. You just accused Vivian of trafficking newborns... Maybe that's the reason for the rule, so she can start accepting bids for the baby.

I got out of bed, hurried over to my laptop, and searched for kidnappings and abductions in Thailand. Pages of results were delivered, and I started reading. There were kidnappings of Thai people and foreigners—all adults. The kidnappings of Thai people were mainly done by family members or someone close to the victim.

However, it was always a mystery when it came to the foreigners. Even the police investigations amounted to nothing. They slowly faded out of the media with no resolution. The victims ranged from retirees to young backpackers. On some occasions, the disappearance was followed by the discovery of a body, but there was no additional information on who killed them. The rest were simply categorized as unsolved kidnappings.

I typed "babies + kidnappings + abductions" in the search field and hit the enter key. A lot of the same articles I had just read appeared. None were of babies being kidnapped. I scanned the results ten pages deep before closing my browser. I wasn't finding my answer through a Google search. If I wanted clarity about what had happened to the Martins' and the Dixons' babies, I needed to talk to people. People who knew them.

Pai and Natti were obvious. The gossip locals were privy to was different from what I would hear. Could Kathy's housekeeper have additional information? It was possible, since Natti was her sister. They must talk among themselves.

But Pai was my best shot, and he worked at my apartment complex. I glanced at the clock; an hour had passed since I left him. Was it too early to go back and try again? He seemed scared. What incentive would he have to tell me what he knew? We weren't friends. When he said 'hi' and asked about my day, it was because he's an employee here, and he's been instructed to do that with everyone.

Emily, are you sure you want to go down this path? You were obsessed with the rules, which led to a distrust of Vivian. Now you're thinking Vivian might have had something to do with the death of Gina's baby, as in abduct and traffic the baby. Wait, is that where we're at right now? Am I seriously connecting the two?

If that was true, I was alone. There was no way I could bounce this conspiracy theory off Jake when he got home from work. He'd think I was a certifiable nut. I wouldn't blame him if he filed for divorce after I gave birth and took the baby with him. Would I dare tell Sasi? She was the only other person aware of my past, but she wasn't bothered by it, maybe because she was in the medical profession. I wouldn't dare bring it up with Jackie or Kimmy. The news would only make its way back to Vivian.

Sasi had told me my mental health was just as important for a healthy pregnancy as my physical well-being. I just needed to hang on. I knew I would never let what happened to Noah happen again. There were precautions I could take to prevent that.

The average pregnant woman would think that wasn't a tall order. But the average pregnant woman hadn't lost a child to SIDS after a difficult pregnancy.

It seemed simple enough if I minded my own business and stayed home. What was more important, my unborn child or being a part of a prestigious friend group?

Just then, my phone rang. It was Sasi.

"I'm so glad you called," I said as soon as I picked up.

"Oh? Anyways, I'm calling because I wanted—"

"Sasi, I'm in trouble, and I don't know who to turn to for help."

"You can turn to me. What happened? Talk to me."

"Can you come over now?"

Thirty minutes later, Sasi messaged me that she was downstairs in the lobby of my building and to come get her.

I went straight down, hooked my arm around hers, and dragged her into the elevator as quickly as possible.

"Emily, what is going on?" she asked.

"Not now," I whispered as I tapped my keycard against the security pad and pressed the number for my floor. "I'll tell you once we're back in my apartment."

That ride up to the fifth floor took forever. I could feel Sasi's eyes boring into the side of my face as I kept my eyes on the changing floor lights. When the elevator doors opened, I hurried her into my apartment.

"Okay, this cloak and dagger act has me seriously worried," she said as soon as I locked the door behind us. "You need to explain fast."

"I'm sorry. I will. Please sit. I think you'll need to."

I started by reminding Sasi about my seeing a therapist and telling her about my issues with Noah's death.

"I know all this, Emily. There's nothing wrong with you. Your reactions are not special unto you."

"I know, but I just wanted to remind you before I tell you the real reason why I asked you to come here because I know I'll sound crazy. Please don't write me off and leave."

"Don't worry, Emily. I'm not doing that. Now tell me."

"I don't think I'm imagining things. I learned something else about other babies born to expat women. I know of two instances where two women both gave birth in the same week, and both of their babies died right after."

"Is this what has you freaking out? Emily, what happened to them is terrible and unfortunate, but your baby is healthy, and your pregnancy is progressing just fine. I don't want you to compare the two."

"But—"

"No buts. I'm serious when I tell you this is not an oranges-to-oranges thing."

"Do you know who I'm talking about? I mean, surely that would be something that would make the rounds in your network of physicians."

"I believe I know who you are talking about. Gina Martin and Beverly Dixon."

"Yes, you know of them. I didn't know Beverly's name, but I knew Gina's. Did you know their doctors?"

"I did, and they are both capable and very good at their jobs. All I can tell you is that those deaths are not connected. It was a wild coincidence and extremely unfortunate. It was investigated, and the physicians delivering the babies were both cleared. So, believe me when I say that what happened has nothing to do with you. Okay?"

"But the babies were cremated."

"Yes, I believe they were."

"Both couples were unaware that was happening."

"Emily, I'm a little confused with where this is going. Are you worried you will give birth and your baby will be accidentally cremated? Trust me, that's not happening. Remember, I'm the one that's delivering your baby. I'm not cremating your baby."

"I know. I'm sorry. I'm not accusing you or anything; it's just that, well, do you think there's any chance something else happened to those babies?"

"Like what?"

"Like maybe they were taken, and the cremation was simply a cover-up."

"What do you mean by 'taken'?"

"Like they were abducted and trafficked."

Sasi bit her lower lip. She looked as if she were seriously rethinking everything she'd told me about my actions being normal. I was sure the next words out of her mouth were going to be that I needed to go back to therapy.

"You think I'm nuts right now, don't you?" I asked. "I know you're thinking that, but I'm not. I have a good reason for coming to this conclusion."

"And what is it?"

"Vivian."

"Vivian? I don't understand."

"I saw Vivian after we last met. She was talking to some strange men and—"

"Emily, I think—"

"Please, let me finish." Sasi nodded at me, and I continued. "I got in touch with Gina Martin's housemaid, a woman named Natti; she was also set to be a nanny for the Martins' baby. Since she was free and I was pregnant, I wanted to talk to her about possibly being a nanny for me. She was on board with everything until I mentioned Vivian's name."

"Why did you mention her name?"

"I can't remember exactly why, but that's unimportant. The important part is her reaction to Vivian. She said that woman was evil and she couldn't work for me if I knew her. She left our meeting immediately without saying another word. I thought there had to be some miscommunication. But I got the feeling she was insinuating that Vivian might have had something to do with what happened."

"Like what?"

"Well, you've been adamant that my mental and physical health are both important for a healthy pregnancy and baby."

"That's right."

"Gina was a part of the same friend group; she was friends with Vivian. And there are those rules, especially the one about pregnancies, so maybe she was stressed out like I am. I mean, clearly, she told them at some point, because she gave birth. But it's no secret that Vivian likes to keep the group small, only four people, and my seat has been a revolving one. Gina before me."

"Was Beverly a part of the group?"

"Uh, I don't think she was, because that would have made the group five. I haven't confirmed that, but I just assumed she wasn't. I know how it looks. How can I blame Vivian for Gina's baby when Beverly had the same thing happen?"

"Thank you for saying it for me."

I realized right then that I had never even considered Beverly's situation or knew anything about her life. I had totally locked on to Gina because of her connection to Vivian. It was as if I wanted to be correct.

"Emily, I think you...well, I think you need to maybe step away from things."

"What things?"

"Everything that's causing you to have these thoughts."

"You mean don't see Vivian and the others."

"Yes. And Natti as well."

"Hold that thought; I have one more thing to tell you. I had a conversation with Pai; he's the guard at the front gate. He noticed my baby bump and said 'congratulations.' So, we started talking. I didn't want him to spread it around, so I told him Jake and I hadn't made an announcement. You know what he said? He said that was a good idea. I needed to keep my baby safe."

"Why would he say that?"

"Exactly, so I dug into that. He knew Gina Martin. He

knew her baby had died, only he said that wasn't true, that her baby didn't die at birth, and that the cremation was a cover-up. He said—and these are his words—'The baby was taken and sold.' Now, I immediately thought that couldn't be right. He must have gotten his words mixed up. So, not wanting the same thing to happen as with Natti, I pressed him for clarity. I asked him if he knew the word 'adoption.' He said he did, and that's not what he meant. He was sure that Gina's baby was taken and sold. I asked him if he thought Vivian had something to do with it."

"Let me guess. He said yes."

"Sort of. He walked away, locked himself in his guard shack, and ignored me. So that's two people who think Vivian had something to do with Gina's baby."

"Do you believe that?"

"I don't know what to believe. I do know that I lost my firstborn, and I do not want a repeat. I don't think Jake or I can handle that happening again. I guess I'm sensitive to any potential problem. Maybe I'm blowing it out of proportion, but Natti and Pai reacted similarly. Pai told me what I guessed Natti already knew or suspected. That's why I asked you to come over. I needed to bounce this off someone, and you're the only person I trust. I can't go to Jake with this. It'll make the problem bigger. Now you know everything I know. What do you think?"

Sasi drew a deep breath as she settled back into the sofa. She wanted to choose her words wisely; she always did. But I also knew she wouldn't lie to me; she'd tell me exactly what she was thinking. I needed to hear a rebuttal, something that said I was wrong. Her eyes shifted to the right as her mind cycled through everything I had told her, carefully weighing the evidence before her. It was that analytical mind of hers that I sought to tap into. Part of me wanted her to agree with my theory, while another part wanted her to tell me I was worrying about nothing.

"I can understand your concern for your baby," she said. "You've experienced something no parent wants to experience. The idea of it happening again is starting to build inside of you and take hold."

"So, your stance is that I'm reading into things?"

"I do think that. You're letting your fears get the best of you, but I'll say it again for the people in the back. I'm your doctor, and I'm telling you your baby is healthy. Everything about your pregnancy is moving along perfectly."

And I'm the one messing it up.

"You need to trust me, Emily. I won't let anything happen to you or your child, so please stop fabricating these worst-case scenarios. You're going to deliver a healthy baby and leave the hospital with him."

"But what about Natti and Pai? Oh, and Vivian talking to those men? I didn't finish my story about them. I saw her."

Sasi waved both hands at me, cutting me off. "It doesn't matter. What does is what you and I do from here on out. We need to be on the same page. Can you do that for me?"

I nodded, because everything Sasi said right then rang through with clarity. I was the problem. No surprise, but I needed to hear someone else say it. Someone who would be objective, like Sasi.

"There's one more thing. I think you should seriously consider it. And that is taking a break from your friends for the remainder of your pregnancy. You mentioned that you were bedridden for the last three months of your previous pregnancy. If you continue down this road, there's a good chance the stress will be too much, and you'll find yourself in bed again."

"Are you serious?" This was the first time Sasi hadn't reaffirmed my situation with positive feedback. "You are, aren't you?"

"That's my advice. It's up to you to decide what you do."

I didn't know why I felt shocked. I always knew that moment would arise. I guess it was easier to forget about it. Out of sight. Out of mind.

"Thank you, Sasi, for being a friend and a caring doctor. You don't know how much I appreciate you." I shook my head as I coughed out a laugh. "I can't believe we're even having this conversation," I said. "It should never have gotten this far, really. With my imagination, I should write a psychological thriller."

Sasi let out a laugh. "That's not a bad idea. Channel those thoughts into a book, and I'll be the first one to buy it."

Chapter Thirty-Five

The following day I woke with a clear agenda: Protect my child. Break the news to the girls.

And...

Even though I'd just had a super-positive conversation with Sasi, I couldn't take the chance that some sort of child trafficking might be taking place. What Pai said was vital in my mind. He and Natti had absolutely no reason to make up a story like that, especially Pai. I still planned on finding out more about what he knew, but for now, I had to focus on how to safeguard my baby.

In my mind, it was better to be safe than sorry. In fact, I wanted to be wrong. That would be the best thing ever. I didn't care if I got labeled as a crazy woman. What was important was my baby. And if I was right, if these connections I'd made were true, then I'd dodged a bullet, and people would have some apologizing to do.

This was where Jake came into play.

As important as it was that Sasi and I were on the same page, for the sake of the pregnancy, Jake and I also needed to work together. From the moment I went into labor to the moment we were home safe with our child, we had to make sure nothing went wrong, i.e., our child wasn't kidnapped.

I had to come up with contingency plans. What if, for some reason, I was put under during the birth? Jake would need to ensure our child never left his sight. He had to understand—strike that, believe—that trafficking was a real threat to us. It was the only way to be one hundred percent vigilant.

How would I convince him that someone was kidnapping newborns? Well, I wasn't quite sure. But I had three months to get him on the same page as me.

I stood nude before a standing mirror and turned to the side, admiring my tummy. My little boy was growing inside of me. And soon, I would hold him in my arms and sing him to sleep.

As for the girls, what had once been a significant concern had become a speed bump on my way to having a child. I could no longer avoid the conversation by wearing oversized clothing in Thailand's hot and humid weather. My fashion choices would only draw additional attention I didn't want. The time to come clean had arrived.

I kept telling myself that I wasn't ending our friendship. I was simply asking for a bit of space for three months. Once the baby arrived, everything could return to how it was. I would want it to. Jackie and Kimmy had children, and their mothering advice would be welcomed.

That's how I'll position it—doctor's orders. Due to my previous pregnancy, I'll need to reduce my contact with others. They had to understand. At least Jackie and Kimmy would.

Worst-case scenario, I piss them off and lose friends. But in return, I gain a healthy baby who Jake and I can love and raise.

When and where I told them would help soften the blow. Maybe while we were having mimosas. They'd be relaxed and open...or they'd turn into angry drunks. Should I do it over lunch? Should I wear a revealing outfit and shout "Surprise?"

The Friend Group

Should I just text them so that my thoughts are in order and I don't miss anything?

Emily, you're overthinking this. It's just the girls. You don't need a plan.

I was right. I shouldn't have had to think it through, but it was vital that it not come across the wrong way. I didn't want the girls to feel slighted. I wanted them to know they were the only people I was telling in Bangkok. I had no intention of making any sort of official announcement. I had always planned on telling just the girls. Everyone else could draw their conclusions when they saw my belly.

Lunch was the most appropriate venue, and we had one scheduled for later that day. We'd be in a public space, so outbursts were out of the question.

Composure.

Composure.

Composure.

I also thought I'd have a little fun with the reveal by wearing a coat, and as I told them, I'd slip it off, revealing the news.

As for the rules, well, I never did confirm any of them. Maybe they were open to interpretation. Either way, I had to get on with it.

We met at one of my favorite lunch spots in Thong Lor, a hi-so neighborhood. Roast was a popular restaurant and always busy, so Vivian and the others would need to keep their cool.

I made sure to get there extra early so that I was the first at the table. If I did that, I could control the situation. Vivian, Jackie, and Kimmy appeared shortly after, all walking into the restaurant simultaneously. Jackie and Kimmy had smiles on their faces. Vivian had daggers flying out of her eyes. Before I could even get a hello out of my mouth, Vivian opened hers.

"Emily's pregnant!" she said as she approached her chair.

Jackie's and Kimmy's smiles shriveled up.

"Wait, what?" Jackie said.

"Is that true?" Kimmy asked as she took her seat.

"Of course it is," Vivian answered for me. "Why she kept it from us? I'm sure the reason will come babbling out of her mouth at any second."

All eyes settled on me, and whatever confidence I'd had when I walked into the place had disappeared.

"Uh, um, I wasn't trying to hide it from you guys. I mean, I always planned on telling you, but in the early stages, most couples wait until they know the pregnancy is secured. That's it."

Vivian made a show about scooting her chair out, so she could lean over to the side and eye my tummy.

"Looks like you could have told us much sooner. What are you, six months now?"

"Um, yeah."

"Congratulations," Jackie said. "I don't care that you lied to us; I'm happy for you."

"Lie? I didn't lie about anything."

"Oh yes, you did," Vivian snapped. "I asked you earlier if you were pregnant, and you said no."

"That's because it was too early to say anything. I'm sorry, it's just that I was pregnant once before, and it was a difficult one. I was bedridden for the last three months and was concerned."

"You already have a child?" Kimmy asked.

"Yes, I mean, had. He passed at six months. SIDS."

"Oh, dear. I'm so sorry to hear that," she said.

"I am, too," Vivian said, still holding a scowl on her face.

"But you could have told us all of this. We're your closest friends here. You should have been able to tell us you wanted to have another child. You should have run it by us."

"Run it by you? I don't know why I need permission. This is a personal decision that is between my husband and me. It's not a group thing."

I could feel myself getting heated, because I had been right. Vivian had meant what she said earlier. But she didn't own me just because she let me into the group. None of them did.

"We do everything together. It's for our own good. As well as yours," Vivian said.

"I'm sorry. I find all these rules a little strange. I get that we want to present ourselves in a certain way, so I'm fine with most of them, but running a pregnancy by you three? Nah, not happening." I pushed my chair out and stood. "I thought this would be a moment for us to come together and celebrate something important in my life. Apparently, I was wrong. I'm taking a break from the group to focus on my pregnancy. Unless you've lost a child, you can't understand what I'm going through right now."

I left quickly, not wanting to give them time to say anything. Plus, if I didn't go right then, they'd see the tears welling in my eyes. I didn't want them to know they'd gotten to me. It took everything I had to leave that restaurant with a dry face. It didn't help that my abrupt departure grabbed the attention of the other diners. I barely made it out the front door before the tears came.

No one came running after me. And I didn't want them to. All I wanted right then was to go back to the apartment. I knew I'd made the right decision. I could not allow Vivian and the others to make decisions regarding my pregnancy.

Later that evening, I received messages from Jackie and Kimmy, but I didn't answer them. I was still angry and sad about what had happened. I felt I needed time away from them for the sake of my sanity. At the very least, a few days.

But after a week, I still felt the same. In fact, I remained angry. What kind of friends make demands like that? That's not friendship. It was more like belonging to a club or an organization or worse, a cult! If that's how Vivian wanted to run the group, so be it. But I was okay with not being a part of it. Because in three months, I'd be busy with my child. All my energy, time, and love would be reserved for him.

Eventually, Jackie and Kimmy stopped contacting me, and I hadn't heard from Vivian since that day in the restaurant. I'd become another friend in the revolving chair and one more point of gossip for people to blab about. And they were gossiping. The staring, the whispering, the looking away when I passed by people I knew—it wasn't lost on me. Word had already spread throughout the expat community. My email and DM inboxes were no longer populated with invitations to attend events. I saw a drop in likes on my Instagram posts and a loss of followers. But those people weren't real friends, so it didn't bother me. The upside was that Jake and I were spending more time together.

"Is event season over?" he asked one night while we were watching television.

"Why, did you hear something?"

"I just noticed you don't go out at night anymore to these galas, not like you did before."

"Oh, yeah. I decided to take a break from all of that for now." I patted my tummy. "I want to focus on more important things."

Jake leaned over and kissed my tummy. "I'm glad you are. I

was a little worried you'd be pressured by your friends to keep living it up."

"No pressure there."

"What do you mean?"

"I should probably tell you I'm not really friends with Vivian and the girls. I hope that doesn't screw things up at work for you."

"What? First, I don't know why you think that would screw things up at work for me. Secondly, did something happen?"

"Remember that rule I mentioned to you about needing permission to be pregnant?"

Jake nodded his head slowly. "Yeah, I remember."

"Well, I was right. When I finally told them, it didn't go over well. Vivian made it very clear that I should have run it by them."

"Like, as in they would give a thumbs up or down?"

"Pretty much."

"So, wait, you're not friends with them now because of that?"

"Yes, because of that. But I'm fine. Our child is more important to me than being invited to events. I was more worried that it would affect your job, being that your boss is Vivian's husband. I take it he never mentioned anything to you."

"No, but it wouldn't matter to me even if he did. You're my wife. Kip is just a guy I work for. I'd back you first on anything. I can't believe they broke off the friendship because of that. It's ridiculous."

I shrugged. "Are you sure everything is fine at your workplace?"

"One hundred percent. Even if Kip knew, I don't think he'd care or even mention it. We're too busy at the office to talk about why you and Vivian aren't friends anymore. And like I said, I choose you over everything, even this job. It's just a job. I can always get another one. I'm glad you broke it off. You don't need this drama, especially now."

I snuggled into Jake's side. "I'm so glad you see it this way."

"Hey, this baby is what's important. You need to be healthy and free of stress. I support you one hundred percent on this." Jake kissed the top of my head.

Real people mattered. And I knew right then who they were: my husband and Sasi.

Maybe this was meant to be. Maybe after Jake's contract was up, we'd move on. Maybe my friendship with the girls was always meant to be temporary and not lifelong. And maybe, just maybe, I wasn't the crazy one imagining shit.

Chapter Thirty-Six

I BALLOONED over the next two and a half months and waddled everywhere. I was carrying more weight with this pregnancy. Sasi was quick to say it was normal. My first pregnancy had been all about avoiding a premature birth. Noah never grew as big as he could have while in my womb. But this baby had every intention of staying inside until the due date.

"I have to say, I like this new you," Sasi said after she finished examining me. "You're happy and worry-free. Taking a step back was smart."

I had told Sasi what had happened with the girls a few days after the blow-up at the restaurant. She completely supported my decision, telling me she thought I'd made the right choice for my baby.

"I can't tell you how happy I am now that my head isn't full of these concerns and overthinking."

"You mean the rules?"

"Yes, those stupid rules. It was idiotic of me to even make a big deal over it. I'm happy to have parted ways with the girls."

"And what about your child trafficking theory?"

"That was me reading into things. I had gone so far down

the rabbit hole I'd lost my way, but following your advice and parting from the friend group solved my problems. I don't even think about it. Oh, and the best part: I'm no longer hallucinating. There is no relapsing. All these issues arose once I became friends with Vivian, Jackie, and Kimmy. I don't know why or how I couldn't see it earlier."

"Sometimes, when we're too close to something, we need someone who's not connected to nudge us. That was me."

"You're absolutely right."

"Do you understand how important your mental health is to all facets of your life, not just your pregnancy?"

"Totally." I slid off the examination chair.

"We have less than a week before you're due."

"I know. I can't wait. I've got that date marked on my calendar."

"Emily, I just want to get this out there. The baby could come early, which is normal. We're well within the window. Or he could come a little later, which again is normal. I'm telling you this just so that you don't focus too much on that exact date."

"I know, I know, but I like it. I see it as a goal, and it's helped tremendously as I cross off days. It reinforces that I'm doing the right thing every day. Plus, if I went into labor right now, I'd be ecstatic."

"I'm sure you would, but until then, keep up the good work. You can always try to revisit your friendship with them after the birth."

"You know, I'm not so sure I want to. I'm fine now, and I'll only be busier with the baby after the birth. I won't want to go to any of those galas, dinners, or store openings. To tell you the truth, I was a little burnt out on them."

"Are you sure?"

I thought for a moment before nodding. "I think so. I've got it out of my system. I'll be able to focus more on my child as I enter a different stage in my life. I'm excited about being a momma."

I left Sasi's clinic feeling as if everything in my life was on the right track. I stood on the sidewalk, waiting to hail a taxi, when I heard someone call my name. I turned and saw Vivian a few feet away.

"Is this where you're going for your prenatal care?"

"Um, I don't see how it's any concern of yours."

"The best medical care is at Royal International Hospital. You know all expats go there for treatment. Why wouldn't you?"

"I think I'm entitled to make my own decisions, and I don't see how it's any of your business anyway."

"It's not, but if you want subpar care for your baby, that is your decision."

"Funny that you say that, coming from someone who knows nothing about my pregnancy. But I'll clue you in. My baby and I are both healthy. There is no need to worry."

"You're taking it the wrong way, Emily. I only wish good things for you."

"What are you doing in this part of town anyway?" I asked. "Seems below your status level."

"Oh please, Emily. If you want to attack me to feel better, that's fine."

"I am not attacking you. I'm simply enquiring." Just then, a taxi stopped. "I'm sorry, Vivian, but I have to go."

I climbed into the car, and just as the car pulled away from the curb, Vivian shouted at me.

"Your baby is in danger!"

Chapter Thirty-Seven

IN A SNAP OF THE FINGERS, all the confidence I had gained, all the happiness I'd been experiencing was wiped away by Vivian's words: Your baby is in danger.

I was a complete mess by the time I got back home. Thank God Jake wasn't back from work yet. Even he had mentioned my improved mood. If he were to walk through the front door right then, he'd see a broken woman in need of treatment.

My past thoughts about child trafficking had come rushing back. Could I have been right all along? Had I moved too fast to clear the slate so I could move forward? It was possible. Sure, I'd felt great for the last two and a half months. All my issues and problems had disappeared. My physical and mental health were one hundred percent. Was that all a façade? Had I simply turned a blind eye to those problems?

If that was the case, then I was back to square one, and what Vivian had said could very well be true.

But what made me even more confused was why she felt the need to utter that warning. Vivian was the reason I had so much stress. She was why I had developed these far-fetched conspiracy theories about kidnapped babies and trafficking. Why warn me?

Was this nothing more than Vivian punishing me for leaving the friend group? If it was, then it was sick and psychotic.

It was a stretch, but I wouldn't put it past her. Vivian was a master at passive aggressiveness. Still, I couldn't imagine her being broken up about our friendship ending. I expected them all to either move on or respect my wishes to be alone for the rest of my pregnancy.

That said, Vivian also wasn't privy to my fears and thoughts about my child. I'd told them about the problems with my previous pregnancy and losing Noah, but nothing about how I thought those other babies didn't die but were kidnapped. In fact, the only person I'd confided in was Sasi.

Sasi had zero relationship with Vivian or the scene she ran in, so I couldn't see how she could be responsible, unless a staff member at the clinic had overheard one of our discussions. I'd become very comfortable there and spoke freely without any concern.

I still hadn't found out how to tell Jake, so Jake couldn't have mentioned it to Kip, with word making its way to Vivian that way.

Emily, you're making up your own answers to your own questions. This is how you get into trouble. If you want to know why Vivian said that to you, you need to ask her.

I couldn't ignore the rational side of me. I'd done that too many times in the past, written off reason in favor of the drama. Not this time. I saw firsthand how toxic my thoughts could be when I let them run free. I created most problems in my life. If the last three months had taught me anything, it was that I did not have complete control over my life.

So rather than spend the day formulating my own theories, I

decided to go straight to the source. I picked up my phone and was about to fire off a message to Vivian when I stopped. This wasn't a discussion to be had via text. I needed to meet with her. I sent a message asking Vivian if we could talk in person. I suggested Starbucks in our community. I had considered inviting her over, but Starbucks was neutral territory. It would force us both to maintain our composure should the discussion blow up. I stared at my phone, waiting for her reply. Vivian was good about answering right away. But this time, she didn't.

Maybe she's pissed and needs time to cool down. But what reason does she have to be angry at me? Unless she's been holding a grudge all these months.

I stopped coming up with theories. It would only worsen my situation. I'd wait patiently for her to answer. Until then, I just needed to hold it together for a bit longer. My baby was due soon. In fact, Jake and I had already discussed him taking time off so that I wouldn't be alone when I did go into labor. We had a plan in place. If my water broke while he was out of the house, I'd call Sasi and then him. I was okay with taking a taxi.

Sasi was more than capable of delivering my baby at her clinic. She had all the necessary equipment, and I wouldn't be the first woman to give birth there. She even gave me a tour of the room where it would take place, just to put to rest any doubts I might have had. I'd been conditioned to think that a smart woman gives birth in a proper facility, like a hospital. Sasi even gave me the option to give birth at the Royal International Hospital, stating it wasn't a problem and that she could easily arrange it.

But the truth is, women give birth in all sorts of places. Home births with a doula aren't that uncommon. I've also heard stories about women giving birth on their bathroom floor or in the back seat of a taxi. I didn't want either of those experiences, and didn't expect to have them. I trusted Sasi and agreed to do it at her clinic.

Everything was set, with one exception. I still hadn't broached the trafficking subject with Jake. It never seemed like a good time, but I knew I needed him on board. I had to make sure we always had eyes on that baby once I gave birth. I didn't want to take any chances.

Just then, my phone pinged. Vivian said she could meet me in two hours. I answered back that I'd see her then. A heavy feeling developed in my tummy. I didn't know why Vivian had that effect on me, like I needed to please her or face her wrath. I was pretty sure *she* wasn't walking into this meeting wondering about a whole bunch of what-ifs.

I drew a breath and then said my affirmations out loud.

"Be strong. You are in control. This is your life. These are your decisions. You do not need approval from Vivian."

I then watched the clock for the next hour and a half while waiting, which only made time crawl. I stepped out on our balcony, hoping for a distraction. One of those long-tail boats zipped by, creating wakes that gently lapped at the canal walls. The pathway below was empty; it usually was. In fact, I hadn't seen any of the girls on it since that one time when we'd first moved in. I thought it was strange. I remembered thinking we'd be having daily walks. We never did, and I never questioned it. I was about to return inside when I spotted Pai walking along the path. He was alone, and I still had time before our meeting. I hurried downstairs.

"Hello, Pai," I called out, startling him.

"Ms. Emily. Hello." He glanced down at my stomach. "Is something wrong?"

"I'm fine, but I'm worried..." I said, my voice lowered to just above a whisper. "I'm worried about what you said about babies being taken and sold. I'll be giving birth soon. How can I stop this from happening to my baby?"

Pai looked up and down the pathway and then up at the balconies above to see if we were being watched. "Ms. Emily, it's not safe for me to talk to you about this."

"I understand, but please help me. Tell me all you know, and I won't bother you again about this." I rubbed my belly. "It's for my baby."

Pai grabbed me gently by the arm and led me to an area where we were hidden under a tree.

"Ms. Emily, all I hear is that babies are taken from white women like you. White-skin babies with blue eyes are in high demand by couples who wish to have a child like this."

"Are these babies taken and then given up for adoption?"

"No, they are taken and sold to these people."

"Human trafficking."

Pai nodded. "The people who do this are dangerous."

"You think Gina's baby was taken and sold?"

"Yes. They make it look like the baby die, but it's not dead."

"Who's 'they'?"

"I don't know, but this has been happening for years."

"Why don't the police do something?"

Pai rubbed his thumb and forefinger together, indicating they were paid off.

"You can't be serious. How can they hide this? What about the parents? Don't they have any idea? I guess that's where the cremation comes in."

Pai nodded.

"But they see the child when it's born, right?"

Pai looked around once more. "Yes, but then they take the baby away."

"You mean the doctor takes it away?"

"I don't know. I only hear this. The baby is taken away, maybe for testing."

"And then after that they tell the parents something happened, the baby died?"

"I think so."

"Do you know how many times this has happened?"

"No, but white babies with blue eyes make money. Many people are involved; it's not one person. Be careful, Ms. Emily. Don't let them take your baby after you give birth. It's easy to disappear in a big hospital."

"I'm not having my baby at the same hospital that all the expat women go to."

"That's smart, Ms. Emily. Keep it a secret."

As soon as Pai mentioned the word "secret," my mind flashed back to Vivian and me outside of Sasi's clinic. She knew that was where I was giving birth.

"Pai, are you afraid of Vivian?"

He nodded quickly.

"Is she involved?"

"I, I think so. I'm sorry, Ms. Emily. I go now."

Pai hurried off, and I wondered if what he said was true. Could she really be involved? Is that why she had the rule about pregnancies, so she could monitor and plan for the real purpose? Which was to sell the baby to the highest bidder?

Chapter Thirty-Eight

After my conversation with Pai, I messaged Vivian, letting her know I had to cancel. She left me on read. I headed back up to the apartment with the intention of staying inside my apartment until I went into labor. If what Pai said was true, I wanted to keep out of sight of everyone.

But Vivian knows where you're having your baby.

And she knew who my OB-GYN was. I could do nothing about that, but that didn't mean Jake and I didn't have control over the situation. It was time to tell him everything. I had the ammunition to make my case. It never did hurt to take precautions. And that was what we were doing. We needed to be vigilant throughout the birth, never let our child out of our sight, and bring him home as soon as possible. If we could do that, we'd be okay.

But just how dangerous are these people? Could they break into the apartment and take my baby by force?

That was a real possibility. Money ruled in Thailand. I wished I had asked Pai if he knew how much money was involved. Was it enough to cover up a break-in and kidnapping of a baby? Would we even be safe in the weeks after I give birth?

Would it make a difference if our child's U.S. citizenship paperwork was filed right away? Did we need to move to a different apartment?

I had lost track of time as I dreamed up possible threats. By the time Jake walked through the front door, I had convinced myself that we needed to leave Thailand right away.

"Hey, sweetie. How was your day?" he asked as he slipped his shoulder bag off. "It's dark in here."

I was sitting on the couch with just the lights from outside coming in through the balcony doors. He switched on a lamp. It took a beat for the smile on his face to fade.

"Is everything okay?" Jake came over and sat beside me. "Is it the baby?"

"Yes, it is. I need you to listen to everything I have to say. Don't interrupt me; just listen. Can you do that?"

He nodded.

I then walked Jake through everything, starting with the rules and ending with my most recent conversation with Pai. I did that so that everything was fresh in his head and we were on the same page. Jake nodded occasionally while I spoke, keeping quiet like I had asked.

When I finished, I studied his face for signs that he thought I was out of my mind. I saw concern, but I couldn't be sure if it was for my mental health or the safety of our baby.

"I'm not relapsing. I'm not crazy," I said. "I know I have an active imagination. I know I go down rabbit holes a lot, but this time, I think we both have concerns. We are so close to having a child; I don't want anything to happen."

"I believe you," he said.

"You do? Are you sure you're not just saying that to placate me? Because if that's the truth—"

"Emily, I believe you. If we must do this to ensure our child's safety, then so be it."

"You believe me?"

"Human trafficking is rampant in Southeast Asia. It wouldn't surprise me if white babies are being kidnapped and sold. It's easy to pay off the police and cover things up."

"Oh my God, Jake. I'm at a loss for words. I thought you would rebuke everything I said based on my past. And..."

"And what?"

His blue eyes locked on me and held my gaze until it was too much to bear, and I turned away.

"You can tell me."

I bit my lower lip, wishing I had stopped while I was ahead. He'd done exactly what I had wanted. And now I'd given him pause.

"Emily?" Jake's eyes found mine again.

I took a breath and let out. "I heard you on the video call when you were talking to my therapist."

"Oh... I didn't realize that. And I can explain it."

"You don't have to. I understand why you made the call. You thought..." My voice trailed off.

"That you were relapsing? You're right; I did. But a few days later, I realized my actions were wrong and unfair. If I thought there was a problem, I should have come to you and not bypassed you."

"Jake, you don't have to explain."

"Yes, I do. I owe you an explanation for my behavior. Had the situation been reversed, and I overheard you, I would have been hurt. I should have talked to you first; you're my wife. I failed to put you first in that instance, and I'm sorry."

I didn't know what to say. I'd never heard Jake share his thoughts that way.

"I also realized something when you were sharing just now," he said. "I can't keep punishing you by bringing up your past. I need to accept that you can move on. Therefore, I must also move on. If I don't, we're doomed to continue living in the past, and I don't want that. I also accept that we're not perfect, and it's okay. I love you, Emily Platt...warts and all." Jake smiled. Those cute dimples of his shined brightly at each corner of his smile.

"Thank you for saying that. Coming from you, it means a lot."

"Look, Emily. You and that child in your belly are the most important people in my life. Nothing will come before you two. If you think our baby's safety is at risk, we must take precautions. It won't kill us to do that whether we're right or wrong."

"So, what part of what I said are you agreeing with?"

"That baby does not leave our sight, not even for a diaper change, until the three of us are home safely. As for moving, I'm not sure I'd go that far yet."

"But what if these people break into our apartment? Wait, do you believe me when I say I think Vivian is...? She knows where we live."

"Let's not worry about Vivian right now. Let's just get the baby home. That's where the other couples failed. If we can do that, we're one step ahead. We have no hard evidence implicating Vivian; it's all hearsay. Kip is a great guy. I find it hard to believe he's married to a trafficker, but with that said, human trafficking is a real problem in this part of the world."

"Well, she might not be doing the actual trafficking. Maybe she's providing the information for a commission. All these people she's connected to in Thailand could be customers. Her role might just be to point out possible kidnappings. Maybe all this time, she's been grooming me. Her husband might not even know."

"You're right. But you also don't know Kip like I do. He's a stand-up guy. I doubt he's involved, even if Vivian is. But taking precautions from here on out until you give birth and we're home safe with our baby? I'm all in. That's what we focus on. Agree?"

"I agree, but are you sure this won't cause problems at work?"

"I'm sure, and if it does, then I'm not interested in that job. I'll get another one. No job is that important."

I had expected to fight Jake every step of the way, but the complete opposite had happened, lifting a heavy weight off my shoulders. I breathed easier, knowing I wasn't alone and Jake was right there by my side.

Chapter Thirty-Nine

From that day on, fears of our child being kidnapped and sold on the black market had been dialed back. I still believed that's what happened to those other babies, even though all I was working with was circumstantial evidence. But like Jake said, it was better to be safe than sorry.

Establishing a protocol for how we wanted things to go up until the birth, during the delivery, and after was the right thing to do. It hurt no one but made me feel so much better. It didn't matter to me if someone thought we were overreacting. We were going on the offensive to protect our child, and there was nothing wrong with that. It was customary to come up with a birth plan. Ours just happened to come from a place where child trafficking was factored in.

Sasi sent me daily messages asking how I felt and reminding me that the baby could come at any moment. She also wanted to know the protocol should my water break while Jake was out.

Jake had wanted to take time off from work to be home with me, but I didn't think he needed to. Plus, the due date was only an estimate. This baby could be two weeks late. Did he plan on sitting around the house for three weeks? He didn't really have a job that allowed him to work from home.

"Okay, you have a point," he'd told me as he got ready for work. "But I'm taking that due date off. My mind's made up."

"Okay, that's fine."

Jake gave me a kiss and left the apartment. I laid in bed for a bit longer, thinking how happy I was that I had listened to my gut. I was pleased that I had the foresight to switch OB-GYNs. I really wanted nothing to do with the expat hospital. I couldn't even understand why women continued to give birth there, but then again, the cover of the babies disappearing was very good. Maybe these women had no idea; if they did, they'd do the same thing I did: have their babies someplace else.

I grabbed my phone and looked up the hospital. I perused the list of OB-GYNs who were on staff. Each physician had a page with a smiling picture and a list of credentials. Their individual pages also listed their schedules. Some were on duty five days a week, and some were only available one day a week. I thought it was strange and wondered what they were doing during their free time. I came across the woman who had been set to be my OB-GYN. I'd only seen her once before switching to Sasi, so I had no real relationship with her. I mean, she seemed nice. Her credentials were impressive. She got her degree in the States and did residency in New York. I was sure she was capable, but if babies were somehow disappearing under the hospital's care, I didn't want any part of it. Really, it was a security issue, not a doctor issue. I was sure all the physicians at the hospital cared about their patients.

I would like to know which of you had Gina as your patient.

I was about to close the browser on my phone when I spotted a familiar face. It was a picture of Sasi.

Why is she on this website? She has her own clinic.

With a closer look, I realized she was listed not only as a

physician at the hospital but also as the head of the OB-GYN department.

Sasi had never mentioned an affiliation with the hospital. Could it be old? Maybe she used to work there before she opened her clinic, and the website just hadn't been updated.

I dialed Sasi right away.

"Hi Emily, is everything okay?" she asked when she answered.

"Hi, Sasi, everything is fine, but I have a question. Do you work at the Royal International Hospital? I was just on their website and saw your photo."

"It's common for doctors to work there part time as well as their own practices."

"So, you still work there."

"No, no. I've scaled back. My attention is now on my clinic. The only time I am there is if one of my patients decides they want to give birth there. Remember I had asked you if you wanted to do that?"

"That's right. It makes sense now."

"Yeah, it's a little different here than it is in the U.S."

"So, you're not in charge of the department?"

"Oh God, no. That's old information. I'm surprised they haven't updated the website. The doctor in charge is a well-known and highly competent OB-GYN. Occasionally, I might consult, but that's as far as my affiliation goes. That's all in the past now. I'm much happier at my clinic. I can run things the way I want to, and I don't have to answer to a bunch of suits sitting on the board who don't know a single thing about childbirth."

"Okay."

"Is there a problem?"

"No, it's just that I thought you would have mentioned it to me."

"Well, there was no reason, I guess, nothing to trigger it. I wasn't trying to hide it from you."

"That's not what I meant. I'm sorry. I've been sensitive lately."

"That's all right. How's your health? Baby feeling good? Any pain?"

"Everything's A-okay."

We chatted for a minute or so longer before ending the call. Sasi had completely satisfied my curiosity. I rolled myself out of bed. I wanted a cup of coffee, and I remembered Jake saying he'd made a pot earlier.

As I neared the kitchen counter, my foot slipped on the tile. I looked down, thinking Jake must have spilled water while filling the coffee pot. The floor was wet, but it wasn't because of Jake. My water had broken.

This is it! It's happening.

Goose pimples erupted across my body as an electric buzzer raced through me. The baby was coming.

Okay, stay calm. There's no need to panic. Follow the protocol. First, call Sasi.

I calmly dialed her number, and she answered after the first ring.

"Emily? Is it time?" she asked right away.

"Yes, how did you know?"

"I'm your doctor. I sensed it this morning. Do you have any pain right now?"

"Not yet, but I expect the contractions to kick in soon; at least, that's what happened with Noah. I think I'll be fine until I get to your clinic."

"Is Jake there?"

"No, he already left for work. I'll call him as soon as I get off the phone with you. Then I'll call for a taxi to take me to you."

"I can send a staff member to come and get you. It might be better than waiting for a taxi. What if they cancel?"

Sasi had made a good point. "Okay, if it's not a problem, I'll take you up on that offer."

"Not a problem. I'm sending someone right now."

"That's fine. I already have my bag packed. I'll be waiting downstairs."

I dialed Jake right after ending the call.

"Hey, what's up?" he asked.

I could tell from the background noise that he was still in the taxi.

"My water just broke."

"Really? Are you sure?"

"Oh, I'm very sure. I've already called Sasi, so she's waiting for me. She's also sending someone from her clinic to come and get me, so I don't need to order a taxi. Where are you now?"

"Halfway to the office, but I'm stuck in heavy traffic. I'm redirecting the driver to take me straight to her clinic. I'll be there as quickly as possible."

"Relax, Jake. I'm not crowning. We have time. I'll see you when you get there, dad-to-be."

"I'll see you soon, mom-to-be."

Chapter Forty

After I got off the phone with Jake, I headed back into our bedroom to freshen up and get ready. I was ready to go in twenty minutes. During that time, Sasi sent me updates on where her staff member was. I collected my bag and headed down to the lobby. Five minutes later, my ride arrived. I recognized the woman; she helped at the clinic's front desk.

"Good morning, Mrs. Platt," she said as she helped me put my bag in the back seat. "How are you feeling?"

"I'm feeling fine and excited. It's been a long nine months."

"Yes, this is a happy time. Dr. Chaidee has everything ready for your arrival. You have nothing to worry about."

"Thank you."

Traffic on the roads that morning was heavier than usual, so we took a series of back roads I wasn't familiar with. I wasn't worried at all. Sasi's clinic wasn't that far from my place. We made a left on a small road, which ended up wide open, aside from a few motorbikes.

"This is my secret way to the clinic," the woman said. "I use it all the time. We should be there shortly. Are you okay?"

"I feel like I have to pee, but other than that, I'm okay."

She made a left onto another street, and as luck would have it, there was a blockade ahead.

"Bad timing," she said as she stopped the vehicle.

It wasn't road maintenance but a line of cement trucks being directed onto the property of a building under construction. I figured once they were in, the men would let traffic pass. Everything seemed to be going as planned as one truck after another turned off the road and into the property.

"Oh!" I said, grabbing my stomach.

"Are you okay?" she asked, looking at me through the rearview mirror.

"I think I just had my first contraction."

"Does it hurt bad?"

"A little, but I'm overjoyed. I'm that much closer to meeting my little boy."

"I think there is only one more truck," she said, looking ahead.

She was right, but this truck was much bigger than the others. The road was very narrow, so it needed to make a series of three-point turns to drive onto the property. Back and forth, the truck moved, achieving inches of progress with each turn.

"Is that truck going to fit into that small entranceway?" I asked out loud.

From my assessment, the opening was too small, and the road was too narrow for the driver to make it into that opening.

"If that driver's not careful, he'll get stuck," I said.

A few seconds later, the truck stopped moving. It was stuck. A group of men gathered around the entrance. They were problem-solving. A few pointed at the walls that surrounded the property. They may have been thinking of removing a section so the entranceway would be wider.

I winced as another contraction hit. It was stronger and hurt.

"Another one?" The woman asked as she looked over her shoulder.

"Yes, but I'm in labor, so it's expected."

Behind us, a line of cars had gathered, so we couldn't reverse out of there. We were stuck and at the mercy of the construction men to figure out a solution. I wasn't panicked or anything like that; surely, this wasn't the first time they'd encountered something like this. It didn't take long before some men decided to disassemble part of the perimeter wall.

"I'm sorry I took you this way, Mrs. Platt."

"It's not your fault. How could we—ouch!"

The contractions were getting stronger and lasting longer, forcing me to slide across the seat to be more comfortable.

"I'm fine. It just feels better if I lie down."

The patience of the cars behind us was starting to fade, and horns blared.

"What are the men doing now?" I asked, as I was too low to see out the window.

"They're still taking down the wall. I don't think it will be much longer."

"Arrgghh!" I yelled out.

I placed a hand on my tummy right below my ribcage and then another on my chest, like Sasi had taught me one day at the clinic. I drew a deep breath through my nose while allowing my belly to push my hand up, careful to not let my chest move, and released the air through my mouth.

"Dr. Chaidee taught you the breathing exercise. Very good."

"Yes, and it's helping."

My phone rang. It was Jake calling.

"Hello," I said between breaths.

"Emily, how is everything? Are you at the clinic?"

"Not yet, but we're close. We ran into some traffic. Where are you?"

"Same. Traffic is hell this morning. I hear you breathing hard; the contractions have started?"

"Yeah, but the breathing exercise is helping... aarrgh! That was a strong one."

"You're doing good, babe. Just keep breathing."

"Soon, we'll see our baby boy."

"I can't wait."

Another contraction hit me, and I told Jake I wanted to concentrate on my breathing and ended the call. I realized the contractions were growing closer, much faster than I had remembered with Noah. There was a little concern, but I knew we weren't far from the clinic. I continued my breathing, focused on managing the pain. My phone rang again; thinking it was Jake, I answered. It was Vivian, and it was a video call.

"Emily, are you in labor?" she asked as she stared at me. I was lying down in the back seat of a car, breathing heavily. There was no lie big enough to cover up what was happening.

"Yes, Vivian! What do you want?"

"I need to be there when you have your baby."

"No, Vivian. I want you to stay far away. Don't even try to come to the clinic. Jake will be there. He'll stop you. We have a plan to protect our baby."

I disconnected the call.

"Is everything okay, Mrs. Platt?"

"Yes, it's fine," I said as I immediately dialed Jake.

"Emily, what's happening?" he said after answering.

"Vivian just called me. She knows I'm in labor. She knows where the clinic is."

"Don't worry about her."

"Jake, she might be on her way there. You need to be there to stop her."

"I will. Nothing will happen to our child. I'll be there to protect you both."

Just then, a powerful contraction hit, and I let out a blood-curdling scream.

"Jake, the baby's coming. I can't stop it. Please hurry. You must get there!"

"The wall is down, Mrs. Platt," the woman said. "The truck is trying to turn again."

An engine revved, and gears shifted. A few moments later, cheers erupted.

"The truck fit. It's driving inside the property," the woman said.

It didn't take long before we were moving again. We made a series of lefts and rights before she announced the clinic was in sight. Relief washed over me as the contractions grew stronger and quicker. This baby did not want to wait.

The car screeched to a stop, and the back door opened. I looked up and saw Sasi staring down at me.

"He's coming," I said. "My legs are cramping now."

"Okay, let's hurry inside," she said.

Sasi and a few other staff members helped me into a wheelchair and rolled me into the clinic as I let out another cry. My initial excitement had waned from the pain. Now I just wanted the baby out of me.

"Is this normal for it to progress so fast?" I asked. "With Noah, I was in labor for eight hours. I feel like I skipped seven."

"Every birth is different, and it seems like this baby wants out now."

I was wheeled into the birth room, and the nurses helped me change into a gown before helping me onto the bed. Sasi examined me.

"Your cervix is dilated at almost nine centimeters. Where's Jake?"

"He's on the way but stuck in traffic."

"If he doesn't get his butt here quick, he's missing the birth."

Sasi and her staff rushed to get everything ready. Before I knew it, my legs were up in the stirrups. Sasi was scrubbed, gloved, and sitting in front of me.

"Emily, it's time. Are you ready to push?"

"I don't think I have a choice," I said as I started to push.

"That's it. You're doing great. Take some deep breaths. Are you ready to push again?"

"Yes."

"Okay. One, two, three, and push."

I gripped the sides of the bed and pushed hard until I couldn't any longer. I relaxed and drew deep breaths. I glanced down at Sasi. She was masked, but I could still tell from her forehead and eyebrows that she was frowning.

"What?" I asked.

She looked up at me. "On three, and we push again, Okay? One, two, three. Push."

I gave it my all for a few seconds before relaxing. I looked at Sasi; she still had the same look on her face. Except this time, she gave a concerning look to one of the nurses.

"What, Sasi? Talk to me!" I shouted.

"Relax, Mrs. Platt," a nurse said to me. "Focus on your breathing."

Another nurse handed a large injection needle to Sasi. "Emily, I need to give you an episiotomy. Your baby is on the larger side. He'll probably be tall, just like Jake. That said, I fear he'll end up tearing you. This shot will numb you, okay?"

I nodded. Sasi waited a minute after the injection and then gave me the episiotomy, which she described as a small incision at the bottom of my vagina.

"There we go. After your child is out, I'll stitch you back up. Okay, are you ready to push again?" This time Sasi had a smile on her face when she asked me.

"Yes, I want to see my baby boy."

I closed my eyes as I mentally prepared myself for the next push. I could hear Sasi counting off.

One.

Two.

Three.

Push!

And I pushed. Again, she repeated her instructions, and again I pushed. It seemed like we were working as a team, each reading the other's mind. I felt as if things were going extremely well. A warmth had overcome my body, something I didn't recall happening with Noah, but it made me feel so relaxed and happy. Maybe it was a birth glow. Whatever it was, I liked it. While I could feel them, my contractions didn't hurt, not like they did with Noah. I thought maybe whatever numbing medicine Sasi had given me was dulling the pain. I kept waiting for my son to appear at any moment, but he hadn't yet. I asked Sasi if I was crowning yet. She smiled at me, and I could sense her lips moving underneath her mask, but I couldn't hear her. I assumed I was. Soon I'd be holding my baby in my arms. At that moment, I felt as if I was on cloud nine. I looked around the room but didn't see Jake. It saddened me that he was missing the birth. The worst-case scenario? He'd meet me and his son at the same time.

I closed my eyes and, on Sasi's instructions, pushed. Again and again, I listened to her and did what she asked. I trusted her one hundred percent to bring me a healthy baby boy.

"Something's wrong!" Sasi shouted.

Wait, what do you mean something's wrong? Sasi? Why is that machine making that noise?

"The baby is stuck; his shoulder is caught under the pelvis."

Stuck? Is that bad? Sasi, why won't you answer me? Look at me; I'm talking to you!

"Prepare the patient for an emergency cesarean delivery."

I watched the anesthesiologist prepare another injection shot.

No, wait. You can't put me under. Jake's not here. We must always have eyes on the baby. Sasi, stop! Vivian is on the way here. She's going to take my baby.

"Hurry, everyone. I don't want to risk the baby suffocating. We must get him out now!"

A nurse removed my legs from the stirrups so that I lay flat on the bed. The anesthesiologist inserted a needle into my hand. I knew I was being given general anesthesia that would put me to sleep, rather than spinal anesthesia, which would keep me awake but numb from the pain. A month ago, I had asked Sasi about this procedure as a precaution. She said if a cesarean birth was necessary, she promised not to give me general anesthesia. So why did it look like I was receiving general anesthesia?

Don't give me that injection. I can't fall asleep. I can't. I must keep my baby away from Vivian.

My eyes were feeling heavy. I could barely keep them open. Sasi had come around to the side of the bed. I had to tell her Vivian was coming. I needed Sasi to help keep my baby away from her. Sasi said something, but it sounded like gibberish to my ears. My mouth moved when I tried to speak, but nothing was coming out.

It's Vivian. She's on her way. Sasi, remember everything I told you. You must keep my child away from her. Please!

Sasi grabbed my hand and leaned in so she could whisper into my ear.

"I promise you, Emily. Your son will be safe. I have a good family waiting for him."

Chapter Forty-One

I OPENED MY EYES, and the fluorescent lights above stung, forcing me to shut them quickly. I could feel someone holding my hand. I forced my eyes back open, just a sliver. I recognized the room. I was still at Sasi's clinic. I turned my head slightly to the side; someone was sitting next to the bed with their head resting in their palm. It was Jake, and it sounded like he was crying.

"Jake," I said softly.

He looked up with red eyes. "Emily. Yes, it's me. Oh, my God. I'm so sorry I didn't get here sooner. I'm so sorry."

"Jake, what happened?"

"I'm so sorry, Emily. It's all my fault."

"Where's our baby? Where is he?"

Jake gripped my hand tighter. Tears were flowing from his eyes. "I'm sorry. He's dead."

"No!!!!!"

I tightened my other hand into a fist and punched the bed repeatedly as I cried.

"No! We had a plan. We had a plan. Jake, listen to me. Look at me."

Jake raised his head and looked me in the eyes.

"Did you see him? Did you see the baby?"

He nodded.

"Are you sure it was him?"

"What do you mean?"

"Jake, did you look at him closely? Did he look like you or me?"

"I, I, saw him. He was dead."

"Jake! I'm not asking you that. This is very important. Did you see him up close or from afar?"

"From afar, but why are you asking me that? It was him. He looked like a newborn that had just been delivered."

"Listen to me, Jake. Our son is still alive. I was right all along."

"What do you mean?"

"Our son was taken; he's not dead. That baby you saw wasn't ours."

Jake's mouth fell slack.

"Emily!" Vivian appeared in the room.

"What are you doing here?" Jake shouted. "Did you take our baby?"

A second later, one of the men I'd seen Vivian with appeared, holding a gun.

"What's going on here?" Jake shouted. "Who are these men?"

Vivian lifted the sheet covering my tummy.

"We need to get her to a hospital. The wound has not been sealed properly."

"What are you talking about?" Jake said as he slapped Vivian's hand away from me. "I saw Dr. Chaidee. She said Emily was fine."

"I don't have time to argue with you, Jake. We must transport her now unless you also want to lose your wife today."

Another man appeared with a wheelchair.

"Help me get her into the chair," Vivian said. "We'll transport her ourselves. It's the fastest way."

"No!" Jake stood, blocking the wheelchair. "I'm not letting you do a damn thing until I know what's going on here."

"Jake," I said. "I was wrong about Vivian, but I'm right about our baby."

"Listen to your wife, Jake. We don't have time to debate this."

"Emily...what's going on?" Jake asked as he looked at me.

"It's not Vivian. It was Sasi. Sasi took our child."

"No, it can't be. I spoke with her when I got here. She explained everything to me. She showed me our boy."

"That wasn't your baby," Vivian said. "It was someone else's, probably kept on ice until today. Now get the hell out of the way."

Jake and Vivian helped transfer me to the wheelchair, and I was ushered out of the clinic. On the way out, I saw more Thai men. The nurses in the clinic were all being held at gunpoint.

"Don't worry, Emily. These men work for me. They'll interrogate the women. We still have a chance to save your child before the exchange happens."

"Vivian, are you saying my son is still alive?"

"He is," she said. "But he's been taken and is being delivered to his new family. There's still a chance to save him, but we must act quickly, or else he'll disappear."

A black SUV was parked outside the clinic, and I was wheeled to it.

"Vivian, you knew about the child trafficking?" Jake asked. "Why didn't you say something? Why didn't you warn us?"

"The people Sasi works with are extremely dangerous. It would be easy for them to eliminate us all and cover it up. I couldn't risk letting them find out we were on to them.

"We?"

"Yes, we. The men with me are ex-Royal Thai Police from their special-ops unit. I hired them to help me investigate the abductions."

Two men popped out of the SUV and helped transfer me into the back seat. Vivian climbed into the back seat with me. She was about to close the door when Jake grabbed hold of it.

"Wait," Jake said. "I don't understand why you are investigating the abductions, and not the police."

"The police are involved, Jake. Now I need to transfer your wife!"

"There must be something I can do?"

"You want to help? Talk to my men inside the clinic."

Vivian slammed the door shut and ordered the driver to leave.

"Why, Vivian?" I asked. "Why are you doing all this? Especially after the way I treated you."

She turned to me. "Because I lost my child to the same people years ago."

Chapter Forty-Two

When Jake first arrived at the clinic, he was met by Sasi. She quickly ushered him into her office.

"Why are we in here?" he had asked. "Where's Emily? Where's my son?"

"I'm sorry, there were complications."

"Complications? How the hell can there be complications?" he said in a raised voice.

Through tears, she'd told him she'd done all she could and was so sorry. Jake's first thought was that something had happened to Emily.

"I'm sorry your baby didn't make it," she'd said.

Those words hit Jake like a sledgehammer to the gut. He simply could not believe what he was hearing. How could this happen twice to them? What had they done that was so bad, so evil, that this tragedy be inflicted upon them once more?

"What happened? I thought her pregnancy was fine."

Sasi explained that there were complications during the birth. The baby was stuck in the vaginal canal, and she needed to perform an emergency cesarean section. The umbilical cord had been pinched, and blood flow was cut off.

Within seconds, Jake had become a broken man, on his knees, one who had now lost two sons before their first birthday.

"I'm so sorry. I did all I could, but..."

"Where is he?" Jake asked.

"Who?"

"My son. I want to see him."

Instead, Sasi offered words of condolence and comfort, but Jake paid her no attention as he sat slumped in a chair, his eyes red and swollen. Suddenly, his expression changed. His eyes narrowed, and his hands balled into fists.

"I need to see him," he said, his voice rising with anger.

"I don't think that's a good idea," she said.

"I don't care if it's not a good idea. Take me to him now!" Jake stood, towering over Sasi. The last of his words echoed through the sterile halls of the clinic.

With a sigh, Sasi nodded. "Very well."

She led the way down a short hallway to a closed Dutch door.

"Wait here," she said as she stepped into the room. She left the top half of the door open. The room looked like a typical examination room. Fluorescent lights running under the cabinets above a long counter were the only lighting in the room. Sasi didn't bother to turn on the ceiling lights.

"We don't have morgue facilities here," she said as she walked over to a gurney. "Are you sure you want to see him?"

Jake took a deep breath and, with a heavy heart, nodded. Sasi flicked on a nearby lamp. She pulled back a sheet and revealed a tiny baby underneath. At that moment, it felt as if the ground beneath him had disappeared as his breath caught in his throat. Jake grabbed the door to steady himself. He'd been so excited to meet his son, to hold him in his arms. But all he felt now was a crushing weight of sorrow and loss.

He had heard Sasi's words, but they hadn't fully registered.

His entire body felt numb as his mind grappled with the shock and disbelief of what had happened. Tears began streaming down the sides of his face. Sasi covered the baby and quickly made her way over to comfort Jake.

"I'll take you to Emily. She's still under anesthesia, but you should be there when she wakes."

"Does she know?" he asked.

"No, she doesn't. You'll need to tell her."

"Okay."

Sasi led Jake to the room where Emily was sleeping. She was lying on a bed, covered with a blanket. She looked peaceful and rested. Jake died a million times, knowing what he'd have to do when she woke. She'd open her eyes and ask immediately for her son. Jake wasn't sure how he would tell her, or if he could. It would kill her to know she'd lost a second child. And Jake couldn't risk losing the love of his life.

"Sasi?" Jake turned around, but she'd already left the room.

Jake took a seat next to Emily. She had no idea what was coming. She'd spent so much time preparing the nursery during the last three weeks. It was perfect, the best ever. She couldn't stop talking about their son. Every night before bed, they would have the same conversations. Who would he look like more? Would he be tall like Jake or short like Emily? Emily had always talked about the idea of their son becoming bilingual. She wanted him to be taught English and Thai, because kids are like sponges, and he'd pick it up easily.

Jake leaned over and kissed Emily on her forehead.

It's my fault. I should have been here. I should have climbed out of the taxi and run over here. I could have done more, but I didn't. I failed you as a husband, father, and protector. Emily, my love, my sweet wife. How can I tell you that our baby is dead?

After the SUV left, Jake returned to the clinic; the women were still being held at gunpoint by one of the men while another was speaking to them in Thai. The man speaking turned to Jake.

"I want to help," Jake said. "What can I do?"

Just then, a third man appeared. He was the tallest of the three and the most muscular. He had a shaved head and a long scar running down the left side of his face.

"You want to help?" he asked.

"I do. I want to catch that bitch!"

"'That bitch' is powerful and very dangerous."

"I don't care. She has my son, and I want him back."

The man snapped a finger, and one of the other men held a handgun out to Jake, urging him to take it.

"Why do I need a gun?"

"Maybe it's better you stay behind and leave it up to us if you're asking that question."

"No. I'm coming." Jake looked over the handgun. "SIG SAUER P365." He dropped the magazine from the grip and looked to see that it was full before locking it back in place.

"You know guns?"

"I grew up shooting. I'm comfortable around them."

"Good. I have two rules if you come with us. Don't hesitate when someone shoots at you. And don't shoot me or my men. Understood?"

Jake nodded.

The man speaking was called Benz. He'd spent twelve years in the special operations units of the Royal Thai Police before retiring. He could make much more running operations in the private sector. Gun for hire was a very lucrative profession.

"Where are we heading?" Jake asked.

He was sitting in the back seat of an SUV next to Benz. The other two men were in the front seat.

"Klong Toei slums. Have you heard of it?"

"I haven't."

"I didn't think so. Outsiders are advised not to go inside there."

"Why? What happens if they do?"

"They disappear. It's easy to get lost in the maze of alleyways. Every turn looks the same."

"What about the police?"

"The slums police themselves; it's too dangerous for the Thai police to go inside. But you don't want their help anyway. We don't know who we can trust. A lot of people make money from trafficking white babies. These people will be angry when we take your baby back."

"Why are you helping? Isn't it dangerous for you?"

Benz smiled at Jake. "The more dangerous the job, the better the pay."

"But how is Vivian connected to all of this? I thought she was responsible."

"Vivian is a clever woman. She approached me a year ago and explained what she wanted to do. At first, I said no because I thought she would disappear once word got out about what we were doing."

"You mean she would be killed."

"Yes, the people involved are powerful and well-connected. But so is Vivian. She's the most connected white woman in Bangkok."

"I'll agree with that."

"You don't know, do you?"

"About what?"

"Her baby."

"She has a baby?"

"She had one, but he was taken and sold, just like the others. She's been working to uncover the players in the trafficking ring since that time."

"Why didn't she go to the embassy, or involve the FBI or even the Royal Thai Police? Surely, not everyone is corrupt."

"Not everyone is, but figuring out who is corrupt is the problem. In Thailand, money is like a drug; once you get a taste of it, it's easy to keep coming back to the well. Before you know it, you can't stop. Greed clouds your judgment and skews your morals."

"Are you saying you haven't been tempted?"

"Everyone is tempted, Jake. Remember that. The slums are not far from us now. We have daylight on our side. If it were night, I'd say kiss your kid goodbye."

"Is just Dr. Chaidee involved?"

"From what we've learned, she's either the ringleader or one of the people in charge. A lot of loyal soldiers working for her are very well paid."

"Sheesh, how much money can one baby bring in?"

"It's not just your baby. Vivian estimates she is trafficking three to four newborns a month from different couples. Thai people, too. It's not just foreigners. People are willing to pay up to fifty thousand dollars for a newborn, especially a white baby like yours."

"Who is buying these babies?"

Benz shrugged. "Rich people. They buy for different reasons."

"I still don't know how something like this can be covered up." Jake shifted in his seat. "So many babies gone missing every month."

"And life goes on. No one cares about your baby except you and your wife. You don't want to hear that, but it's true."

The SUV slowed and then turned off the main road and parked.

"The slums are down this block. The entire area is only 260

hectares. I believe, in your country, the equivalent would be a square mile."

"It's not that big."

"No, but more than 100,000 people are packed into that space, and they're all opportunists. Having you here gives us an advantage."

"Oh yeah? And what's that?"

"You make good bait."

Chapter Forty-Three

VIVIAN HAD DRIVEN me straight to the expat hospital. During the entire ride, she never let go of my hand. She kept telling me everything would be okay and not to worry about my baby. The men she had hired were very good at what they did. But not once since she appeared at the clinic did she mention what had happened between us or the accusations I had made about her. Her only concern was my health.

"Vivian, I'm sorry. I knew about the abductions and the trafficking. I thought. I thought it—"

"We're almost there. The doctors know we're coming and are ready."

"Do you hear what I'm trying to say?"

"Yes, I hear you, and I know you thought I was involved. I don't blame you. But I couldn't tell you anything. All I could do was keep an eye on you. We'll discuss this later."

"I'm sorry, Vivian."

"Emily, we're friends, and sometimes friends fight. But that doesn't mean we stop being friends. Right now, what's important is getting you proper treatment. That doctor left you at the clinic to die. You've lost a lot of blood."

The car stopped in front of the hospital's emergency room, where the staff was waiting, just like Vivian had said. Within seconds I was on a gurney being wheeled down a hallway.

"Vivian!" I called out.

"I'm right here." She appeared, walking beside the gurney. "Jackie and Kimmy are on their way here. We'll be waiting for you."

Vivian fell out of sight as I was wheeled through a pair of double doors and into an operating room. A nurse in a crisp white uniform hooked me up to an IV and vitals monitor while another covered me with a medical sheet. A man placed a mask over my face and told me to take deep breaths and count backward from ten. I got as far as seven before blacking out.

I woke in a recovery room. Gray drapes were drawn shut on either side of my bed, but I could hear hushed voices on the other side. I groaned, and a second later, the curtain opened. It was Jackie, and behind her were Kimmy and Vivian.

"Oh dear, how are you feeling?" Jackie asked as she took my hand and gently squeezed it.

"The doctor said you're all fixed up good," Kimmy said. "You'll just need a week or so to recover."

"Are you in pain?" Jackie asked. "Do you need some drugs? I can ring the nurse."

I shook my head. "Water," I whispered.

"Yes, of course," Kimmy said as she darted over to a table and poured water into a cup from a plastic container. "Here you go, dear." She held the cup to my lips and tilted it gently. The cool water provided relief for my dry throat. I took a few more sips before pulling my head away.

"Did you all know?" I asked, my voice still a little raspy. "About the trafficking?"

"They didn't know," Vivian said as she moved closer to the bed. "They only found out when I told them you were in surgery. If you want to be angry with someone, direct your rage toward me."

"I'm so sorry," Kimmy said. "I couldn't imagine having something like this happen to me. I, I..."

"I'm with Kimmy," Jackie said. "It's tragic, and I want you to know all three of us are here for you. Anything you need, you can count on us."

I nodded at both Jackie and Kimmy before looking at Vivian. She cleared her throat.

"It's time I told all of you what happened to me. When Kip and I arrived in Bangkok ten years ago, we were novice expats. Thailand was our first overseas placement. Adapting to life here with no guidance was more than an adventure. Back then, the expat community was a fraction of what it is now. There was no one to teach me how things worked, so I learned largely by trial and error. Part of that error was meeting people I thought I could trust but never should have. People took advantage of my generosity in ways I never would have imagined. There was a time when I felt like an ATM. But I learned how to read people, and I sharpened my skills. The one thing I wish I'd done back then was question more. Everyone went to the Royal International Hospital like they do now because it's what everyone did. Had I done my due diligence, my outcome might have been different. Maybe I'd be a mother right now."

"But you told me to go there," I said. "You insisted I go there."

"I did, but it's not because of what you think. Ever since my baby was kidnapped and sold on the black market, I'd been focused on two objectives: Find my child. Find the people who took him. I've only made progress on the second objective." Vivian removed a tissue from her purse and dabbed at an eye.

"But how did you figure out your child was abducted?" Jackie asked.

"I'd heard rumors that newborns were being abducted, but at the time, that's all it was—rumors. The police were useless when I tried to tell them what I thought. Turns out they were involved. Like other women before and after me, I was told there were complications at birth, and my child died. I was still trying to process his death when I was informed he was cremated. I wanted to die at that point because I never got to look at him. To this day, I don't know what he looks like."

Kimmy put an arm around Vivian and hugged her. "I'm so sorry to hear this."

"I was a basket case, but I figured I could either wither away in sorrow or focus on finding out what happened. I had no proof something fishy had happened. It was just my gut, a mother's instinct. Kip accepted what had happened with our child and was prepared to move on, but I couldn't. From that moment on, everything I did, every decision I made, was done to uncover the truth."

"And that's how you became the Vivian you are today?"

"Yes, it was an unforeseeable result that played to my advantage. I learned that the trafficking ring was extremely complex and run by powerful people who were connected. A lot of money is made from it, which is why the cover-up is so seamless and successful. It's the reason why this absurd cremation excuse works. Because it's impossible to challenge. No one listens to a grieving mother claiming foul play. But to answer your question from earlier about why I would insist you go to an expat hospital, that's because I had fully vetted and cleared the OB-GYN assigned to you. I could trust her. I can't say the same for the others."

"Did she know about the abductions?" Jackie asked.

"She did, but it was too dangerous for her to let on that she knew. In the past, some brave doctors tried to sound the alarm, and those doctors disappeared. Don't worry; any care the four of us receive at the hospital comes from vetted physicians. This goes for our family members as well."

"Thank God," Kimmy said. "I still can't believe all this is taking place right under our noses."

"It's better that way. Anytime someone starts to pull back the curtain, they disappear. In this situation, the less you know, the less of a threat you are. That's the reason for the secrecy."

"Is that why you insisted on the pregnancy rule?" I asked.

"It is. Had I explained it to you, you would have written me off as a lunatic right away. You might even have told others, and the next thing you know, there are waves. These people running the trafficking ring don't like waves. That's why the rules of our group are so important. I can't watch out for everyone, but I can watch out for my friends and their loved ones. I know this all sounds bad, but telling you three everything could have put us all in danger. In fact, we could all be in danger right now. This is why I tried to keep it from you three."

"Are you serious?" Jackie clasped her hand across her mouth.

"Let's not panic. I have capable men working for me," Vivian said.

Vivian explained how she had hired them a year ago and the progress they'd made together in the last year.

"I was screwing everything up," I said. "I can see how I was making waves. Is this why you were following me?"

"Wait, you were following Emily?" Kimmy asked.

"I felt I had no choice. I'd discovered that Emily was being targeted. There was a lot of, what do you call it? Chatter. If I'd mentioned any of this to you, I couldn't be sure how you would react. I already knew you were hiding your pregnancy because of the rule. I don't know if I made the right choice by keeping you in the dark as long as I did, but I had to make decisions. And anyway, you were already making waves on your own."

That's because I have an active imagination, I overthink everything, and I have a history of psych problems. But in this instance, with some of my theories I was spot on, while dead wrong on others. I had the girls, especially Vivian, all wrong. But I was right about the craziest idea of them all, the child trafficking angle. Of course, the one person I had trusted throughout my pregnancy was the biggest danger.

"I can't believe Sasi stole my baby," I said. "I trusted that woman."

"Sasi is the OB-GYN, right?" Kimmy asked.

I nodded. "I switched to her because I thought I could trust her."

"How did you find her?" Jackie asked.

"I met her at a little farmers' market."

"Your meeting wasn't by chance," Vivian said. "I think she sought you out."

"But I wasn't even pregnant at the time we met."

"I believe the ring keeps tabs on everyone, so the minute someone is pregnant, it's easier for them to move in. The minute Sasi found out you were pregnant, it was over."

"She's very good; I never once suspected her to be a threat. Even when I complained about you guys—sorry, I was stressed—she never told me to drop you guys. She suggested I take a break, but mostly she just listened."

"And that made you trust her even more."

"That's right. I can't believe she was playing me the entire time." Tears welled. "And now my baby is on the black market, probably being handed over to another couple. I can't believe I failed another one of my children."

"You didn't fail anyone," Vivian said. "You were targeted by professional traffickers. They're very good at what they do. Part of that is identifying and pushing a person's hot buttons relentlessly."

"Oh, my God! Where's Jake?" I suddenly remembered we'd left him at the clinic.

"He's with my men."

"You need to call them and tell him to get over here. He has no idea how dangerous these people are. He could end up getting killed. Please, Vivian. Call them!"

"I'll call them," she said, removing her phone from her purse. "Just calm down. I don't want you to rip your stitches."

Vivian rang her guy, and a beat later, he answered. "It's Vivian. Is Jake Platt with you? The tall white guy? Wait, where are you? Are you crazy? Get him out of there! It's too dangerous!"

Chapter Forty-Four

BENZ LED the way down a narrow street with Jake beside him. Jake could already tell that he was out of his element, and it didn't help that he was a tall white guy. He might as well have had a neon directional sign pointing down at him.

"That was Vivian," Benz said as he got off the call. "She wants you to stop helping us and go to the hospital."

"Not a chance in hell," Jake said.

"Suit yourself."

Jake wasn't terribly worried at the moment; the place looked like a typical market with vendors selling fruits and vegetables. But within a few steps, the crowd thickened, and he soon found himself rubbing shoulders with the locals in the maze-like alleys of the slums. Makeshift shanties, built from scraps of corrugated metal and wood, protruded into the narrow passageways, giving it a claustrophobic feel. The stench of garbage mixed with the pungent aromas of street food didn't help matters.

The deeper into the slums they went, the more the air became thick with the sound of clanging metal and the hum of generators powering various small businesses in the area. The locals eyed Jake suspiciously as he passed by. A small group of children played barefoot in an open space, kicking a soccer ball around. A few tagged along, tugging at Jake's shirt.

"Don't encourage them," Benz said as he shooed them away. "They work for the gangs, and their job is to determine your value."

"Seriously?"

Benz stopped walking and turned to Jake. "Don't let the daylight trick you into thinking it's safe here. Listen to everything I tell you, or I will not be responsible for what happens to you. Clear?"

"Yeah, sure."

"This whole place is self-sufficient. Everything the people need they can find here. See that man in the white coat sitting on that chair?"

"Yeah."

"He's a dentist."

"Where's his office?"

"It's that chair. Like I said, self-sufficient. They also police themselves. Judgments and punishments are given by the residents to those who do wrong." Benz continued walking.

"You said earlier there are gangs in here."

"There are, but even they have a code of conduct. So long as you don't act like an idiot or stick your nose where it doesn't belong, you'll be OK. Believe it or not, the Klong Toei market is a popular place for Thai people to buy fresh seafood."

"Really? I hope the fish isn't fresh out of those nasty, litter-filled canals. Anything else I should know?"

"Yeah, if you hear whistling—a lot of whistling—then you need to get the hell out of here as fast as you can."

"Why?"

"Because it means you've been marked. Marked people rarely leave the slums."

"This place just keeps getting better and better."

"I admire you, Jake. Most people would never have come in here with me, but you are here, even with what I just told you."

"I'm here to get my son back. If there's a chance, I have to take it."

Benz nodded. "You have a chance."

"You think he's still alive?"

"Yeah, dead babies don't pay much. Until the exchange is made, great care and precautions are being taken with your child. The customer will not purchase a sick or injured baby."

"So, say we find my son, then what? Surely, they aren't just handing him over."

"No, we must take him, most likely by force. According to her staff, Dr. Chaidee has your son. She's meeting the buyers here, a wealthy couple from Singapore. Once both parties agree on the sale, money is transferred, and the couple takes ownership of the baby."

"Then what?"

"They probably have a private jet waiting for them. We need to stop the exchange, or you can say goodbye to your son forever."

"Have you done this before? I mean, stopped a sale."

"No, this is the closest we've come to cracking the trafficking ring. But we learned a lot from the staff back at the clinic. Dr. Chaidee is the brains of this entire operation."

"Great, we're walking into this blind." Jake ran his hand through his hair. "We're fucked."

"I spent twelve years in special ops. This isn't, as you call it in America, my first rodeo. I'm not getting shot, but I can't say the same for you." Benz pointed to the handgun I had tucked in my waistband. "Don't be afraid to use it."

"Will my or my wife's life be in danger whether I get my son back or not? I want an honest answer."

"Probably not. Vivian survived all these years, and she's been digging into this operation for a while."

"Is her husband, Kip, aware of what she's been doing?"

"Who do you think is paying us?"

Benz pressed a finger against his lips, hushing Jake. Only then did Jake realize the area had become quiet. *Where is everyone?* Jake realized the residents were doing their best to remain out of sight, but they were there. Everywhere he looked, he saw prying eyes staring at him. An old man smiled, showing off his missing teeth. He fashioned his hand into a gun and pointed it at his head, then pretended to shoot himself as he laughed.

"We're close," Benz said as he ordered his men to split off.

"What's the plan?" Jake asked.

"Dr. Chaidee is here someplace. It's too risky for you to be walking around. She might recognize you. My men will scout the area ahead and try to pinpoint her location and tell if she still has your kid. For now, we wait."

Jake crouched down next to Benz. They were hidden from sight behind a stack of rusted metal barrels. He kept his gaze fixed on the ramshackle cluster of shanties up ahead that Benz had pointed to. Sweat dripped down his neck, dampening the collar of his shirt. He didn't think the day could get hotter, but it had. The buzzing of flies didn't help, but at least his nose had numbed to the smell of sewage that hung in the air when he arrived.

Benz removed a tiny pair of binoculars from his shoulder bag and observed for a moment before putting them away. He then tapped out a message on his phone to his men. A few seconds later, one pinged him back.

"They think they found her," Benz said. "We need to move closer."

Benz pulled out his handgun, prompting Jake to do the same. Slowly and silently, Jake followed Benz through a narrow passage, keeping to the shadows. They approached a large shanty and positioned themselves directly under a window. A cloth drape covered the window, but they could hear a hushed conversation inside. Jake recognized a woman's voice speaking English.

Benz sent messages to his men, letting them know his location. One of his men reported they had the front door in sight. Two armed men were standing outside. His other man was located to the left of the shack. He had a view into the place through a tiny window. He confirmed that Sasi was inside but couldn't tell if the baby was there.

"The deal is in progress," Benz whispered. "That means your baby is inside the shack."

"Are you sure?"

Benz took a moment to think. "No. There's a chance the baby is being held close by while they negotiate. It's impossible to tell right now."

Jake needed confirmation. He slowly inched his way up until his eyes were at the bottom of the windowsill. The tattered curtain blew gently, most likely from the rotary fan he heard blowing inside. He carefully parted the curtain from the side of the grimy window, just a sliver, enough to peer inside.

The inside was dimly lit, with only a single flickering bulb casting a yellowish glow. His eyes fixed on the back of a woman's head—he recognized her as Sasi. She sat at the rickety table opposite an Asian couple, who nervously shifted in their seats.

His blood boiled as he realized what was happening. They were still negotiating the sale of his baby. Jake clenched his jaw in anger as he listened to Sasi speaking casually; she even chuckled as she placed a hand on the woman's hand to make her feel at ease.

That bitch!

But nowhere in the dilapidated shack did he see his baby boy. Was he being held elsewhere, as Benz had suggested? Jake lowered himself.

"She's negotiating, but I don't see my son."

"Then your baby is nearby in another shack."

Jake nodded. "Maybe we wait for the sale to go through and follow the couple."

"They'll have armed bodyguards escorting them. Right now, we have the element of surprise. We need to take advantage of that."

"So, what are you suggesting?"

"We need Dr. Chaidee alive," Benz said. "She knows where the baby is. Everyone else is expendable."

"Are you serious? What about the couple?"

"They are not innocent; they are buying your baby."

Benz sent instructions to his men.

"Stay here, Jake; let me and my men do our jobs. Okay?"

"Okay."

Benz disappeared around the corner of the shack, leaving Jake alone. Gripping his gun tightly, Jake drew a deep breath as he crouched below the window, his heart pounding in his chest.

Suddenly, gunfire erupted from inside the shack, the sounds echoing through the narrow alleyway. Jake instinctively covered his head as bullets punched through the flimsy material of the shed, sending splinters of wood flying in all directions. Fear surfaced inside of him as he realized how dangerous this mission was.

Jake had to know what was happening inside. He popped up and peeked inside the window. The single light bulb he'd seen hanging earlier swayed frantically back and forth, casting harsh shadows. The woman's husband lay partly on the table, blood seeping from a wound in his head as his wife screamed at the sight. A figure—a woman—scrambled frantically toward the window. It was Sasi. Did she see him?

A bullet whizzed by Jake's face, forcing him to drop to his knees. A second later, Sasi tumbled out of the window, landing hard on top of him, knocking the wind from his lungs. Jake quickly regained his composure and found Sasi sprawled beside him, gasping for breath. There was surprise in her eyes as she stared back, or was it fear? Jake still held his handgun. Like clockwork, he pointed it at Sasi.

"Where is he?" Jake demanded, his voice cold and steady. "Where's my son?"

Sasi laughed, a heartless shrill that raked at Jake's ears. "You think you can threaten me? I run these slums."

"Don't think I won't shoot you." Tightening his grip on the gun, Jake knew the situation didn't favor him. He'd made a false threat. Could he really shoot Sasi in cold blood?

"Shoot me, and you'll never see your child again," she spat back at him.

But then, from out of nowhere, a woman appeared with a bundle in her arms. Was that his baby wrapped up in a blanket? Jake's heart leaped with joy and relief as he reached out to take his son. But Sasi quickly snapped at the woman, threatening to kill her if she handed over the child. But the woman ignored the threat and continued her steps toward Jake to deliver the baby to him.

Sasi placed two fingers into her mouth and blew hard. A piercing whistle echoed in the alleyway. Benz's haunting warning returned to Jake as he realized what had happened. Sasi whistled again, much louder this time. In the distance, Jake heard others answering the call with more whistling.

The woman holding the baby pointed at Sasi and then at Jake's gun. "Shhhh," she said.

The doctor continued to whistle as more joined in, creating

a cacophony of deafening alarms. The woman holding the baby urged Jake again by tugging on the arm holding the gun.

Bang!

The bullet slammed into Sasi's forehead, silencing her as she fell back onto the pavement, vacant eyes staring straight up. The woman shoved the bundle into Jake's arms, and between the folds of the blanket, he spied a tiny baby looking up at him with blue eyes. The woman pushed Jake, pointing down an alley just as more gunfire erupted.

Jake ran.

Chapter Forty-Five

JAKE WASN'T OUT of the woods yet. He was now a marked man lost in a maze where every turn looked exactly like the last. The alleyways would spin him around into a continuous loop if he wasn't careful. The canals were his only hope. He knew from his walk into the place that they flowed in and out of the slums. Following one was his best shot at getting out.

He held his baby tightly against his chest as he hurried forward, checking every few seconds to see that his son was okay. He wasn't crying, which Jake took as a positive. But at the same time, he feared for his son's health. He wasn't even a day old. What were his chances of picking up a disease in the rat-infested slums? Surely cholera, typhoid, malaria, and more ran rampant in the place. Was his immune system strong enough to fight?

The whistling continued to echo around. Jake knew he was being watched from doorways, windows, and shadowy nooks. He had no idea if Benz or his men had survived the gunfight but hoped they had.

Up ahead he spotted a canal; he wasn't sure which one it was, as they also all looked the same. He turned right when he reached it and ran forward, nearly tumbling to the ground as a dog darted out into his path.

The residents were also becoming bolder, standing in his path as they whistled. Jake held his baby like a football tucked against his chest, leading with his shoulder as he barreled through anyone who stood in his way. He still had his gun, but the last thing he wanted was to shoot his way out. He couldn't risk the chance of someone shooting back and hitting his son.

The canal veered to the right up ahead, and Jake spotted a small skiff anchored at the bend. He was confident he could remember his way back out from that point on. As he rounded the corner, he ran into someone. Jake was about to push through until he realized this person was pointing a gun at him.

"Look, pal. Take my wallet. You can have everything inside of it; just let me go."

The man looked at the bundle Jake held against his chest and motioned for Jake to give it to him.

"Sorry, I can't do that. It's not happening."

Jake heard a hammer being cocked as another armed man appeared directly behind him. He was sandwiched between the two, and while he was still armed, it bought him no advantage. He might be able to fire a round into one of the men, but he would take a hit, and perhaps so would his child.

"I've come too far to simply hand over my son. I don't know if you can understand me, but there must be some deal we can work out." Jake then said the Thai equivalent of money. "Ngein?" Sensing it had caught the man's attention, he repeated it. This time the two men looked at each other.

The man in front of Jake said something in Thai, but Jake didn't understand what he said as he spoke too fast, but it had to be about money. Jake threw out a number. "Hmun dollars." Ten thousand dollars seemed reasonable, and Jake knew he could transfer the money right then and there on his phone.

"Sam, hmun," the man fired back.

He wanted thirty thousand. Money wasn't the issue, but Jake knew he didn't have that much cash to cover a transfer on the spot. And asking for a few days so he could shift money around wouldn't cut it.

"Song hmun dollars," Jake said this time, upping his offer price to twenty thousand. He showed off his watch, indicating he'd add it to the deal.

The man wanted a closer look, so Jake slipped the timepiece off his wrist and handed it over. "Rolex watch," Jake said. "A lot of ngein. No fake."

The man examined the watch before shoving it in his pocket and saying, "Sam hmun." He still wanted thirty thousand dollars.

The way Jake saw it, no matter what he gave them, they weren't letting him leave. They were just shaking him down for everything he had. With a crowd beginning to gather, Jake saw his chances of escape diminish. Some bystanders were still whistling, maybe calling for more people to show.

A commotion from the rear of the crowd grabbed Jake's attention. A few men were making their way to the front. It was Benz and his men. Jake was about to breathe a sigh of relief and tell Benz his timing couldn't have been more perfect when he noticed Benz didn't share his enthusiasm. Instead, he drew his handgun and pushed it directly into Jake's face, ignoring the armed men shaking him down.

"What are you doing, Benz?"

"Remember when I told you everyone can be tempted?"

Those words slammed into Jake, knocking the wind out of him. He stared at Benz, his eyes wide with shock and disbelief. How could this be happening? He had trusted Benz with his life and had risked everything by following him into the slums. And now he was being betrayed right when it mattered most.

As he struggled to make sense of it all, Jake's mind raced back through their time together, searching for any sign of deception. But there was nothing, no hint of the double-cross brewing beneath his nose. Had he been so blinded by his desperation to save his child that he had missed the warning signs?

The reality of the situation hit Jake hard. His hopes of leaving the slums alive with his child were deteriorating. Jake looked Benz straight in the eye and said, "You made a big mistake. And I promise you, somehow, you'll pay for it."

"Tell me about it." Benz retrained his gun at one of the armed men and fired, striking him in the face. Benz's men shot the other armed man. The crowd surrounding them scattered like roaches in a kitchen when the lights were switched on.

Jake choked on his breath as he stared at the two dead men, a pool of blood spreading beneath them.

"What? Did you really think we double-crossed you?" Benz asked.

"I, I..."

"Save your apologies for later. That trick I pulled only works once. We have a small window to get out of this smelly shithole."

Chapter Forty-Six

VIVIAN and the girls insisted on staying by my side until I was released. Vivian even arranged for a guard to be posted outside my room just in case trouble arrived. All I could think about was Jake. Was he alive? Was he able to track down Sasi and get our baby back? Vivian had sent multiple text messages to the man she'd hired to help her crack the trafficking ring. She hadn't heard anything since she last spoke to him and found out they were heading to the Klong Toei slums. I'd never even heard of the place. But after hearing her describe it to me, I wished Jake never went. I didn't think I could handle it if I also lost him.

"Benz is a good man. I trust him," Vivian said. "He's extremely well trained and has been on countless operations, all successful. Trust me, I vetted the guy hard before I hired him."

"I still can't believe you actually hired men to take on this trafficking ring," I said.

"If I didn't, they would continue to do what they're doing with impunity. Plus, revenge is a great motivator. I just hope it pays off. There's no turning back now. All my cards are shown; they know I'm on to them. It's all or nothing. But believe me when I say this, above all, I want nothing more than to have your child returned to you."

"Thank you for everything you've done, Vivian." I gave her arm a gentle squeeze. "I know I've already asked you this a million times, but can you try your guy again?"

Vivian nodded. "Of course."

"Keep the faith, Emily," Jackie said. "Vivian did a job that nobody in Bangkok was willing to do or could do."

"I second that," Kimmy said.

"Oh please, I had a lot of help. The biggest coming from my silent partner, my husband."

"I can't believe he let you do this," I said.

"It wasn't easy. He fought me tooth and nail in the beginning, but he saw that I would have no peace if I didn't follow through. He gave in, but with rules. We agreed to tell each other everything, and he had an ace in his back pocket. If he ever felt it was getting too dangerous, he could pull it out, and I'd have to stop. Believe me when I say there were many times when he reached around for that card."

"I bet."

Just then, a commotion on the other side of the door, men speaking loudly in Thai, grabbed our attention. A second later, the door opened, and in walked Benz, followed by two other men. But I didn't see Jake, and my heart sank. Benz must have noticed the look on my face because he turned around immediately and looked out of the room. A second later, he stepped off to the side, and in walked Jake, smiling. And he was holding something wrapped up in a blanket.

"Emily!"

"Jake!"

He hurried over to me and placed the blanketed bundle into my arms. I had already heard the cooing before I'd seen his face.

I pushed the blanket off to the side and saw my baby boy staring up at me, and he started to cry immediately.

"I don't know if I should take that as a good sign," I said.

"He might be hungry," Jake said. "I have no idea if he's been fed."

Jake was right, because he latched right on to me without any help.

"My God, isn't he precious!" said Jackie as she came around to the side of the bed.

"He's absolutely adorable," Kimmy added. "Those blue eyes are to die for."

"I'm calling the doctor," Vivian said as she got on her phone. "We need to have him looked over."

"Jake, I can't believe you got our baby back."

"We have Benz and his men to thank, as well as Vivian and Kip. If they hadn't been working on cracking this ring... I don't even want to think about it. I'm just glad we're all safe."

"I haven't heard you guys call him by his name yet," Vivian said. "He does have a name, right?"

"We had it narrowed down," I said, looking at Jake, "But I don't think we made a final decision, did we?"

"I think you're right, but I'm still thinking neither of those names feels right, especially now."

"I agree," I said as I looked down at my little bundle of joy. He looked like he was in heaven. "We're going to take a few more days to give it some thought. I hope you're okay with that. We just want you to have a name that suits you well. You're our little tiger, raaawwwrrr."

Chapter Forty-Seven

Tiger.

That's what Jake and I decided to name our little guy. It seemed apropos, considering Tiger had spent the first day of his life on the run.

As soon as the doctors looked over our little guy and gave the thumbs up, Jake and I left the hospital. I still needed bed rest for a day or so to help the cesarean wound heal, but I didn't need to be in the hospital for that to happen.

Jake hired Benz and his men to watch over us at our apartment in case of any fallout. As far as we could assess, Sasi had been the ringleader. Benz did a lot of digging around, doing his best to name her accomplices. He said it was important to let those who'd been working with Sasi know they no longer had anonymity. He said as much as those people loved the money, they cared even more about saving face, and their social standing. The trafficking ring constituted a white-collar crime here in Thailand. The people involved would rather walk away than be connected.

Within a day, any connection Sasi had had with the Royal International Hospital was scrubbed from the website, along with the names of three other prominent OB-GYNs suspected of working with her. The fallout didn't stop there; ten other staff members at the hospital who were alleged to be involved were arrested by the police, which was interesting to me because Sasi's criminal enterprise would never have worked had the police not been willing participants. The powerful and the rich got away, leaving the less fortunate holding a big pile of shit. All in all, it never came out that there was a large trafficking ring operating in an elite profession. It was just quietly swept under the rug.

The government shut down Sasi's clinic immediately, citing a series of health violations; her staff was rounded up and never heard from again. As for Sasi herself, word was put out that she had gone on the run, and the Royal Thai Police vowed to capture her and bring her to justice no matter how long it took.

That might be a challenge, considering Jake had shot her dead in the Klong Toei slums. Benz told us not to worry about it. The slums policed themselves. The body was probably already cut into hundreds of tiny pieces and fed to whatever was hungry in the canals. The residents in the slums who had been involved with Sasi would simply move on, looking for the next big meal ticket.

Was there justice? Not in the Western sense. We got our baby back, and that was what mattered to us. Would we have wanted to see Sasi locked up for life? Nah, I liked that the last thing she saw was Jake firing a bullet into her head. She deserved nothing more and got what was coming to her.

Jake and I had no complaints about how things ended. Sure, back in America we would have figured out whom we could sue, but we were in Thailand. An eye for an eye was how things worked. We could have ended up being another statistic. We considered ourselves lucky.

But were Jake and I any better than they were? We had

gotten even through our own brand of vigilantism. We'd operated freely outside of the law. Did that make us like Sasi and her gang? I guess it depends on how you look at it, but I don't think we would have gotten Tiger back if we had simply filed a missing persons report.

Jake invited Vivian and Kip for dinner a few days after we returned home. He thought it was important to let them know personally how much we appreciated everything they'd done. Their loss years ago was what had saved our child. And we wanted them to know we were sorry for their loss yet grateful for their persistence in chasing their own brand of justice.

Jake held up his glass of wine. "I want to propose a toast. To Kip and Vivian, two of the most solid and genuine people I have ever known. Emily and I are forever indebted to you. Anything we can do to repay the favor, the answer is yes. Thank you both for being... well, for being just the nicest couple. We love you."

"You two aren't the only ones who are thankful," Vivian said. "Being able to finally catch the person responsible for taking our child is something we don't think can ever be repaid. Thank you two for trusting and believing in us, even when we were the last people you thought you could trust."

"Did you ever suspect it was Sasi?" Jake asked.

"Not at all. She wasn't even on my radar," Vivian said. "Kip and I were both convinced it was someone at the Royal International Hospital."

"That makes total sense; that's where most of the expat abductions occurred."

"If it wasn't for Emily switching to Sasi, I don't think we would have had a happy ending. We got lucky. Sasi's secret weapon was her ability to stay under the radar. She could have continued this racket for as long as she wanted. For the past eight years, I estimate she sold thirty to forty babies a year."

"I can't believe no one stopped her earlier," Jake said.

"There was no one fearless enough who wasn't corrupt," Kip said. "Until my wife got involved." Kip put an arm around Vivian and kissed her on the forehead. "She's a stubborn woman, and I'm proud of her."

"To Vivian!" I said, raising my glass.

"To Vivian!" the others chimed in.

Later that night, Vivian and I had a chance to talk one-on-one while Jake and Kip sipped old and expensive Scotch out on the balcony.

"I'm sorry, Vivian," I said for the umpteenth time.

"Emily, you don't have to apologize. I would have thought the same thing you did."

"Why did you keep it secret? I mean, I know why you kept it a secret. You've explained it to me a million times. I guess what I'm getting at is it could have gone a different way."

"You're right. Things could have gotten worse. I don't have an answer for you, because I wasn't always sure if I was doing the right thing. But I knew I needed to operate under the radar if things took a wrong turn. Emily, we don't always have the best reasons for doing things, but we do have our best intentions. Sometimes that's all we have, and we hope for the best."

That night, I found a new admiration for Vivian. I'd never met anyone quite like her, and I was sure she had never met anyone like me. I learned that we all have our imperfections, and we deal with them as best we can in a way that only we can understand. It doesn't need to make sense to others; it only needs to make sense to us. I learned that my active imagination could either run the show and turn me into a liability, or I could manage it and use it to my advantage, regardless of what others think. My so-called conspiracy theories would have had people judging me and writing me off. But you know what? My gut, the one I always thought was insane, had been right.

Sasi had always told me not to judge myself too harshly and

that a lot of what I thought was wrong with me was normal. She was right in the sense that every one of us has skeletons in our closets. It's just that some of us are better at hiding them. Sasi was certainly a pro at that. She was the most normal psychopath I'd ever met.

Click to read Timber: Peter Darkwood is worried about his wife, Timber, a renowned artist who has settled into depression. To help her rekindle her passion, he hires Mitzi, a life coach. But things take an unexpected twist as Mitzi delves deeper into Timber's fragile psyche and learns about the chilling secret she's been hiding.

A Note From Ty Hutchinson

Thank you for reading THE FRIEND GROUP. If you're a fan, spread the word to friends, family, book clubs, and reader groups online. You can also help get the word out by leaving a review.

Join my Exclusive Readers Group to receive "First Look" content, and information about future releases. I'll never spam.

I love hearing from readers. Let's connect.
www.tyhutchinson.com
tyhutchinson@tyhutchinson.com

Also by Ty Hutchinson

Abby Kane FBI Thrillers

Corktown

Tenderloin

Russian Hill (CC Trilogy #1)

Lumpini Park (CC Trilogy #2)

Coit Tower (CC Trilogy #3)

Kowloon Bay

Suitcase Girl (SG Trilogy #1)

The Curator (SG Trilogy #2)

The Hatchery (SG Trilogy #3)

Find Yuri (Fury Trilogy #1)

Crooked City (Fury Trilogy #2)

Good Bad Psycho (Fury Trilogy #3)

The Puzzle Maker

The Muzzle Job

Fire Catcher

Not A Safe Place

Psychological Thrillers

The View from Nob Hill

It Ends Now

The Friend Group

Timber

Sterling Gray FBI Profiler

Hunting the Mirror Man

The King Snake

The Butcher of Belarus

The Green Samurai

Sei Thrillers

Contract Snatch

Contract Sicko

Contract Primo

Contract Wolf Den

Contract Endgame

Dumb Move

Clean House

Done Deal

Mui Thrillers

A Book of Truths

A Book of Vengeance

A Book of Revelations
A Book of Villains

Mui Action Thrillers

The Monastery

The Blood Grove

The Minotaur

Darby Stansfield Thrillers

The Accidental Criminal
(previously titled Chop Suey)

The Russian Problem
(previously titled Stroganov)

Holiday With A P.I.
(previously titled Loco Moco)

Other Thrilling Reads

The Perfect Plan

The St. Petersburg Confession

This book is a work of fiction. Names, characters, places, and incidents are the product of the author's imagination or are used fictitiously. Any resemblance to actual persons, living or dead, is coincidental.

All rights reserved. No part of this book may be reproduced, stored in a retrieval system, or transmitted in any form or by any means (electronic, mechanical, photocopying, recording, or otherwise) without the prior written permission of the author, Ty Hutchinson.

Published by Ty Hutchinson

Copyright © 2023 by Ty Hutchinson

Cover Art: Damonza

Printed in Great Britain
by Amazon